HUM

Emily Bullock won the Bristol Short Story Prize with her story 'My Girl', which was also broadcast on BBC Radio 4. Her short stories have been included in collections such as *A Short Affair* (Scribner, 2018). She has an MA in Creative Writing from the University of East Anglia, and completed her PhD at the Open University, where she teaches Creative Writing. Her debut novel, *The Longest Fight*, (Myriad, 2015) was shortlisted for the Cross Sports Book Awards, and listed in *The Independent's* Paperbacks of the Year. Her second novel, *Inside the Beautiful Inside*, was published by Everything With Words in 2020.

ALSO BY EMILY BULLOCK

The Longest Fight
Inside the Beautiful Inside

Human Terrain

Emily Bullock

REFLEX PRESS

First published as a collection in 2021 by Reflex Press
Abingdon, Oxfordshire, OX14 3SY
www.reflex.press

Copyright © Emily Bullock

The right of Emily Bullock to be identified as the
author of this work has been asserted in accordance
with the Copyright Designs and Patents Act 1988.

All rights reserved. No part of this publication may be
reproduced, distributed, or transmitted in any form or
by any means, including photocopying, recording, or
other electronic or mechanical methods, without
the prior written permission of the publisher.

A CIP catalogue record of this book is
available from the British Library.

ISBN: 978-1-9161115-9-2

1 3 5 7 9 10 8 6 4 2

Printed and bound in Great Britain
by Imprint Digital

Cover image by Lightspring/Shutterstock.com

www.reflex.press/human-terrain/

For Charles

CONTENTS

My Girl	9
Tombstoning	17
Pig Lady	25
Zoom	41
Dinner Dance	47
Freshwater	49
Human Terrain	57
We Want It Out	63
Things We Did When We Were Children	67
On Broadway	77
They Were the Only Ones Dancing	79
Back Issues	87
A Glimmer of Melting Ice	91
Fences	105
Open House	115
Shoots and Weeds	129
The Jam Trap	133
Somebody Said	141
A Match	155
Beginnings and Endings	157

My Girl

My job is to stop the blood, cool her off, wash her down. Who knows her better than her own mum? I rub the yellow carwash sponge across her head, smooth my fingers over the braids, sweeping away water with the back of my hand. Her coach leans over the ropes, whispering words I can't hear. All I have to do is make sure the match isn't stopped for bleeding. I open a jar and rub adrenaline chloride into the cut on her right cheek. Old scar tissue has ripped open, isn't much blood, but I'm not taking chances. My girl keeps her eyes on the other corner, but she lets me move her face from side to side, checking for fractures. Clean. An eyelash drops and curls onto my finger. I make a wish and send it on its way. The bucket of icy water has clouded pink, but her reflection is steady. Nobody hears my wish.

Time is nearly up. I collect the bucket, towel, and my toolbox of potions. I sit back down on the other side of the ring where it is darker, small pools of pale light collecting under the lamps on each table. I am one of them again: spectator. My girl stretches her arms and legs, letting the ropes take her weight, in the last seconds of rest. But the ring isn't empty. The men cheer as the bikini-bulging girl, slipping in her white sling-backs, parades with the second-round card held high above her yellow perm; howls loud as dogs left chained in a backyard, the air cold with moans.

I rub blue sanitiser into my hands. I don't want any dirt to get onto her broken skin. The liquid evaporates quick as tears; it smells tart as the gin and tonics splashed across the tablecloths behind me. This is an exhibition fight, but the money is good, and it will keep her in gloves and membership for six months. My girl watches it all. She shakes her head, and water hits the floor in front of my shoes. The man behind me orders another round of whiskies and a cheer goes up.

The bell for the second round deadens the noise for a moment. My girl comes out tight, keeping hits away from the red lump swelling above her kidney. Her opponent is a swarmer. She comes at my girl again, happy to take hits on the ride in. Whisky splashes against my neck as a man behind waves his glass in the air. But my girl is fast. She blocks the blows without turning; eyes watching her opponent's muscles. Ready to knock and duck. Bang. My girl lands a punch to the side of the head. She circles and steps off again.

Reach for it, reach for it, a man screams from behind his stack of pints; myopic eyes blinking through the glass.

No backdoor nightclub scratching and slapping here. Some cheer, and some snigger behind napkins as they dab steak juice from their lips. Swift footwork smears blood into the canvas, pinned shadows the fighters move around. A left uppercut to her opponent's chin silences the crowd. Splatters of red spin over the ropes and smack the front row; a spot balloons on my jeans. The other fighter's knees lock, a real pro, and stays standing. She pulls back, elbow in for power, and slugs my girl deep in the gut. I can't breathe for her, can't feed her from my body anymore. Her eyes narrow and she circles; playing for time as she sucks down air to free the hot cramping pain. Her blue singlet and shorts turn black with sweat. After the fight, tonight, I will tell her. Enough. My girl took the punches even when she was a swollen bulge inside me.

It was a blow to the stomach finally woke me up. I was expecting it, my hands wrapped around her hidden body, leaving my head uncovered. He raised his foot above my face, but something stopped him: the banging from the neighbours upstairs, a siren on the street. He slammed the hallway door so hard it bounced right open again, did the same with the front door. I held on to the broken back of the chair, sat up, and felt my girl kick. I laughed: all those doors wide open.

A draught from the fire exit blows litter in off the street, a crisp packet and burger wrapper circle and settle by the bucket. I boot them away. The cold air is no good for her muscles, but no one will hear me if I shout at them to close it again. The green light glows through the grey soup of smoke and beer belches. I shake the clean towels, plumping air into the folds.

They are locked together, tugging apart at the referee's shout. Her heart is fair beating out of her chest. She snorts air, nostrils flaring. But she isn't slowing. Her lip doesn't droop; her eyes aren't blinking. It is a good sign. Her coach signals with his hands, their secret language: a combination of hits or a change of tactics. She won't tell me their code. And that makes me proud. I'm here because she wants me. She's long past needing me to pull up her socks, wipe her nose, trim her crusts. So I wait for the bell to go, fold my bandages, mix my ointments to stop the cuts flowing. Hands working automatically as I watch her spin and circle around the ring. Her stretched plaits reveal the soft pink of her scalp; fontanelle toughened over the years, but I remember the first warm pulsing.

On the 18th of December 1989, when waves smashed Blackpool pier and leaves whipped against windows, she began to fight. In the upstairs bathroom, on a blue fish and smiling-dolphin beach towel, the ambulance delayed under a falling oak, my girl was born. She came out screaming: fists balled, face red, breathing hard. No one but me to hear her.

The bell goes for the third round. I am back at her side again. I squirt water into her mouth; collect it in the bucket as she spits it up. Wipe down her face and grease her skin to make the leather slide off. My nipples throb under the layers of jersey just like they did when she was a baby. I press a frozen eye iron to the top of her cheek, milking out the swelling. She lets me cradle her head but tilts her ear towards the bell to better trap its sound.

She catches a couple of good hits in the third. One to the ribs. One to the back. A small cut is opening up under her right eye. It will need seeing to. She is hooking with her left, and some of the men lean forward shouting encouragement, congratulating her coach. She's a born fighter, he tells them and waves his hand to show it is all he has to say.

I stood outside the gates on her first day of school, parents waving all around. And she asked me, What happened to my daddy? He was a fighter, I told her. If there were ever words I wish I could swallow back, they are it. The bruises he left me had long since yellowed and leaked away. She didn't ask anything else, and I knew she'd get smart enough to fill in the rest. I watched her swing her orange PE bag over her shoulder, and I waved until I thought my hands would drop off.

The fluorescent strip light coats her with its orange glue. With a right uppercut, her opponent stuns her. I see her eyes as they flicker white. She glances over. All I can do is sit back and let it happen. The other fighter presses closer, forcing my girl's curling spine up against the ropes. Bang. Bang. Bang. A burst of hooks so fast, I'm not sure if I count three or four. But my girl won't go down. The light swings above the canvas, dividing up the ring, as they circle each other. Matched pound for pound, my girl stands an inch shorter than her opponent; but she meets her in the eye like they are the same height. No one has ever come close to knocking her down. Not that it stops me biting my lip and holding my breath.

When she was seventeen, out of school and out of work, she found her way to the gym. The boys there said, "Er's a funny 'un.' She didn't listen to them and went back every day it was open. She asked Bristol Pete, shoplifter-to-order, to fetch up some Everlast leather gloves, ten ouncers. I used to worry that she never came home until the sky outside the kitchen was one dark bruise, that welts and scrapes on her skin glowed red in the cold night air. I only let myself exhale when I heard her key in the lock. On Sundays she ran along the cold, sucking sand, jumping dog shit the tide wasn't quick enough to wash away.

She swells in and out of the other fighter's reach, keeping in close and holding her guard up. My girl feints with a left and follows through with a smack from the right. She doesn't stay still to soak up the praise from the crowd. Feet seeming to float above the canvas as she pushes towards a neutral corner. My girl is punching smooth and fast, legs wide enough for balance but close enough that the petroleum jelly at the top of her thighs has rubbed off. Her skin will be turning red under those long silk shorts. My girl gets up close, ready to finish it. But her opponent isn't down yet; feet shuffling, shoulders dipping as she comes back at my girl. A deep blow under the belt, but they are too close, their bodies block the referee's view. Only I see it. That burning pain in her groin is spreading through her legs, slowing her down. She can't lower her hands, can't press the spot to deaden the pain. I crack an ice pack and get the water bucket ready. One sneaky left hook and bang, it could all be over for my girl too. Some punches in life you can't slip.

They're calling her The Blackpool Illuminator because she lights up the ring; that's what she told me over egg and chips, runny not set, a week before her first match. I knew why. It wasn't in her face, square and blunt like mine, or her hardened body. It was in the way she moved. Fork to mouth, knife to plate: stabbing out combinations, left and right. She pushed off from the balls of her feet as she got up to help me with the dirty plates. My girl balanced like a spinning top. I held my wrists under the cold water until I managed to squeeze out a smile for her.

The ice pack in my hand is numbing my skin. But I suck down hot air, whistling through my front teeth, as my girl takes a jab to the side of the face. Her head snaps back on her neck as the end bell goes. For one moment, I taste the frozen silence of the hall, it fizzes and crackles on the heat of my tongue. But it isn't a sugared ice lolly taste. The points are totted up. The white-shirted referee lifts an arm. Of course, the hometown fighter wins. Her fist smacks up into the air. The cheers aren't for my girl. Not this time. She slaps gloves with her opponent and crosses the canvas, back to me. But I keep my arms stiff at my side so they can't open wide and pull her close.

Sweat runs into her eyes, and she tries to flick at it with her gloves. I hold back her head and wipe her face dry with a fresh towel; press the ice pack to the base of her neck. I dab at the small cut under her eye; red and yellow, congealing already. Maybe if I hadn't wiped over her beginnings with that word, fighter, if she wasn't born in the great storm of '89, she wouldn't be up there now. But I can't imagine her any other way. Her opponent is carried off in a whirl of white-teeth smiles, and pumping arms. The audience is leaving, scraping chairs and slapping backs. I rub her down with the towels, cloak her body and legs. The men tug on jackets, sleeves turned inside out, fingers numbed by booze, and legs deadened from steak and chips.

'I'll bring the car round,' her coach says as he gives her shoulder a pat.

A lone flashbulb bleaches her face. It's all done for the night.

'I lost,' she says.

'You didn't win this one, but there'll be others,' I tell her.

There won't be any story about my girl in *The Echo*, not tomorrow anyway. Search for her online and boxer puppies for sale from Blackpool kennels pops up. I hold open the ropes, and she climbs out of the ring. She breathes in the coppery smack of blood, the taste of success. Together we walk through the blue ticket-stub, crumpled napkin dust that the dinner jacket men have left behind.

Sometimes we aren't the hero in our own stories: she fights, and I stand in her corner, is the way it will always be. Fists balled, face red. Breathing hard.

Tombstoning

Danny wasn't just a drug addict; Danny was a vegan. Once he even made us take the bus into town on a hunt for condoms. The normal ones use lactose, he said. He loved animals, chatted about them all the time. There are a million ants in the world for every human; there's a species of jellyfish that reverts to childhood after becoming sexually mature, making itself immortal; some seagulls have learned to save energy by hovering over bridges to absorb rising heat from the tarmac.

I know all sorts of things because of Danny.

He didn't just talk about animals; he used to draw these cartoon scrawls of tortured rabbits and beagles. I don't mean they were bad, they were good, really good, but in a twisted, scratchy, mangled way. Every market day he'd drop off a load with the anti-vivisection lot outside Boots. There must have been about fifty drawings each week because the pile always made this slapping noise as it hit the plastic-covered table, fluttering up their leaflets. They never put one of Danny's drawings on display.

All the art and the trips into town, that was before Danny got into drugs. Hard stuff. He'd been smoking weed since primary. We met in year three. Danny didn't really have friends, but him and me hung out at the bus station after school, and sometimes we'd meet up on the weekend. I can't remember why. Danny was the sort adults crossed the street to avoid, and kids only went near if they wanted to score. He had a smile that showed both rows of teeth, his bottom lip curled under. A smile to remember all the more because I only saw it once.

I hadn't thought about Danny for years before I opened the post this morning. My mum often sends me cuttings from the *County Press*. Weddings and births: people I don't remember and those I've tried to forget. There isn't even a note with the cutting I've just unfolded. The paper's thin like old skin, ragged at the edges where Mum must have given up on the scissors and ripped it from the other pages. A couple of printed paragraphs circled over and over with red Biro. I imagine Mum sitting at the coffee table, pressing hard enough to leave tracks in the wood. I bet those twenty lines are the most anyone's ever written about Danny.

I know why Mum sent it.

Christmas just gone, on my yearly visit back home, she found a teenth of Thai stick in my rucksack. I only took the ten-bag with me to take the edge off crossing that narrow stretch of the Solent. You might know the place, a little island off the south coast: clean beaches, green hills, award-winning ice cream, and penny slot machines lined back to back. If you've been, it was probably a day trip or a week with your school – Outward Bound, climbing ropes, and orienteering in the dark. But when the grockles and festival hipsters go home, winter always sets in early. I don't live there anymore. It's for the best.

Don't get me wrong, I'm not blaming Danny; he's not the reason I left. I've barely thought of him over the years, although I've never forgotten that day on the bridge. The seagull. All the trouble Danny got in, which is saying something because he was used to trouble.

He came into school one time, screaming about how he was going to kill us all. Turned out someone had stuffed dog shit through his letterbox. All I said was, Hi, Danny. And he hit me, right on the nose. After I got up, and my head stopped vibrating, I remember being pleased. Danny didn't see me as a girl, not like everyone else. You can still see the break, if you look closely, like a fissure in weathered tarmac.

Island roads are different – that's what he did with the vegan condoms, filled them with piss, threw them from the top deck, aiming at those road signs all the way home.

He lived in a terrace, two-up-two-down, with his dad: proper old man, older than all the other dads. But that's what a lifetime of Bell's whisky for breakfast does to you. That row of terraces is a Morrisons car park now. The first time I went there was with my mum, helping her with a Christmas shop. I remember sitting in the car (about where his kitchen would have been) and wondering where Danny had ended up. Now I know.

Back then, when Danny wasn't in that dump of a house, he used to hang out at the bus station off season, and in summer he could be found on Coppins Bridge. There are better places to go for a dip when it's hot, but the beaches throb with holiday-makers lying on dumb blue and pink dolphin towels, drinking Nescafé from polystyrene cups. Us local kids stuck to the river.

Every summer I'd lose some flip-flops to those gluey black mud banks. Sometimes at low tide, you'd see an old pair sticking up like the wings of ditched model aeroplanes. We all wore the same uniform of baggy jeans, hooded tops and flip-flops. Not Danny, he wore his school clothes: blue trousers and grey shirt, the tie gone – because it was the holidays after all – and clunky soled shoes. He never wore socks, claimed he liked his feet to be free. It wasn't until years later that Danny started shooting heroin into the soft flaps of skin between his toes.

I won't tell you where Danny got the heroin from – it's a small island, you probably already know. We all knew, even back then. Just like we knew Danny could score weed from his older cousin.

Danny turned up at my place once with his hair shorn right off. He asked my mum if she could tidy it up; she was a hairdresser, not a miracle worker. He left with a belly full of McCain's oven chips and a little pot of Vaseline to rub into the nicks. He told me later his cousin did it when he found out Danny had been selling-on his weed – it was just for family, the cousin said. It was one of those families you find rooted in the cracks of small places, who don't find it small enough, keeping themselves clenched together. Danny was the only kid in our class who'd never been on a ferry to the mainland. I sort of wish I'd given him the money for a day return now, but what difference would that have made?

The day of all the trouble started bright enough. We must have been about fourteen. Danny and me stood on Coppins Bridge, not where the roundabout is but farther up where the tarmac arches over the river. There's a point in the middle of the bridge where the Medina runs dark. We leaned over the railings, like looking into the mouth of... of something deep. Barges had long since stopped delivering to the quay, and it was too far away from Cowes and its deck shoe, Helly Hansen-wearing yacht types to have any boats passing under. But still we had to time it just right; a bit of mud bank could be showing but not the mooring rings. Danny nodded at me. It was going to be now.

No one else was jumping. Cars and caravans drove past in a shimmering kaleidoscope of fumes. The midday sun sizzling up shadows. Danny trod on the heels of his shoes, kicking them aside. I slipped off my flip-flops. The tarmac was sticky and hot. We climbed onto the top railing, thick enough to balance on; a squared imprint burning into the soles of our feet. The temptation was to spread your arms like wings. I stuffed my hands in my pockets, locked my knees, held my balance. Danny kept his fists clenched to his sides.

Jump – that's all you had to do. But it took some kids days to build up to it. Not Danny, he went in first time, every time. I followed.

Stepping into nothing.

For a second it all fell away. Floating; seagulls spinning past. But it couldn't last. No time to stand straight as a tombstone. A cold blast of air whispering up from the river like a hissed warning.

We hit the water: a thud like the iron railing whacking against our feet.

Sinking. All breath thrust upwards: bubbles whirling towards the surface. Trousers sucked against hips, T-shirt trying to escape over arms. Dragged deeper by the cold current. Struggling under the weight of ourselves.

Danny was much heavier than me, but he burst to the surface first. His white soles a ghostly glow above me. I forced my way up, gasping.

Floating on my back, staring into the sky. A bang rang out, scattering the seagulls. Something splashed into the river. I swam to the side. Danny was already out, a puddle evaporating about his feet. He leaned against the quayside railing, the shadow from the bridge touching him. I climbed the steps behind him.

Danny's cousin and two mates stood beside their dirt bikes. Revving to drown out the sound of another day dripping away. Dust and grit swirled about their ankles. Deep tracks scored into the embankment where they'd driven the bikes down from the bridge. The cousin rested an air rifle on his hip like a cowboy. The mates juggled a chunky black shoe and a pair of flip-flops.

The cousin said, 'These yours?' He didn't wait for an answer. 'Throw,' he shouted as he bumped the rifle into his shoulder, aiming up.

The mate with the red baseball cap threw Danny's shoe into the air. The seagulls dipped and trembled then jerked up as if attached to invisible strings, high into the sky. Three shots, but the cousin never came close. The shoe splashed into the river. He tried again with my flip-flops but didn't hit them either.

The other mate, the one with the bleached hair said, 'What we going to shoot now?'

The cousin rubbed at a spot on the barrel. 'Could see which one of them makes it to the bridge first. Danny or his little – you a boy or a girl?'

I crossed my arms over my damp chest. The mate with the red cap picked up a stone, threw it at Danny; it hit his leg. 'Hey, kid.'

Danny didn't answer. He stared up, trance-like, at the gulls. I'm sure he never achieved such a reverie state again until he took a hit of his first speedball. He swept a hand over his stubbly head, splattering water. I wanted to go home, burning up in my own skin standing there on the tarmac. But that's when Danny said it,

'If I hit a gull you've got to give me the gun.'

His cousin laughed. The mates egged him on. It was just like any number of other days in any other number of seaside places, where something to do was better than the lifetime of nothing squeezing the breath from your lungs. The deal was done. The air rifle handed over.

Danny raised the gun, aiming at the back of the flock. A black-headed gull tipped its wings from side to side, going nowhere.

A crack echoed under the bridge, but there'd only been one shot. The bird plummeted. Thwack, it hit the dirt in front of the bikes. I don't think anyone thought Danny would make the shot. The gull lay still, wings spread, body bloodied. A breeze lifted the broken flight feathers on its tail.

His cousin took a step towards the carcass; the bike leaned in too. The mates peered at the seagull dead on the ground. The one in the baseball cap slid it back from his forehead; the other one rubbed his chin.

Danny stood tall as his cousin came towards him, holding out his arm. But he didn't shake. He pulled back, punched Danny in the gut, catching the rifle as Danny reeled back.

Danny clutched his sides, panting. 'You said you'd give it me.'

His cousin laughed. 'You're not getting nothing.'

Danny wiped his hand over his mouth, smearing a streak of red; he must have bitten his lip when he doubled over. He spat more blood onto the sweating tarmac; some hit the white feathers. Danny bent down, reaching for the lifeless gull, gripping it in his hand.

The bird seemed to fly once more before it hit the cousin's face: rolling down his T-shirt, landing on his trainers. He flicked and kicked the carcass into the water. Danny took his chance, snatched the rifle back, embraced it. His cousin punched him in the chest, but Danny held on. The cousin kicked at his shins, but Danny didn't go down. He held on tight.

The baseball cap one said, 'Let the kid have it.'

'Deals a deal,' the bleached one said.

'Piece of shit doesn't shoot straight anyway,' the cousin said, stepping away.

Danny raised the barrel above his head. And he smiled with all his teeth on display.

Well, someone driving over the bridge must have seen the rifle and called 999. The gun got confiscated. The RSPCA prosecuted. Danny didn't need court and cell time. There was a fine too; I don't suppose it ever got paid.

They sent Danny to special school after he got out of young offenders.

That day on the bridge wasn't the last time I saw Danny, but it is the last time I remembered until those paragraphs in the *County Press*. I rub my finger over the lines. The cheap ink smudges, but it doesn't change what's written there.

They found him in a bedsit, at the back of the bus station, above the model shop. Apparently, for a day or two, there was some excitement that he might have been done in (there aren't many murders on that small island), but it turned out to be an overdose. The article said Danny was a drug addict. My mum underlined it, three times.

There is a funeral. I won't go. I don't suppose many will.

But that day on the bridge, Danny looked happy even as he spat blood at our feet. He beat us all, you see. That day on the bridge, Danny smiled.

Pig Lady

After the lunchtime rush, she would pull up outside in her Transit van. Rick would always call out, 'Pig Lady's here.' She didn't seem to mind being called that. It's what she was after all. She would come in with a big black bin over her shoulder, carry it through the chip shop kitchen, slap it down by the store cupboard and wait for me to bring her out the day's leftovers. Sometimes she'd say, 'The pigs are much appreciative.' But usually she'd say nothing at all. Being so often with pigs, she probably didn't find much need to chat.

She always wore this padded body-warmer, a sheet of dark green plastic stitched to the back panel. Must have been to stop the bin juice soaking down to the bone. Her jeans were for men, easy to tell because she wasn't too careful about buttoning the fly, and her boots were probably for men too as her feet were quite a size. I joked once, 'I'll hand you down my waders when I'm done with them.' I wore white fish-fryer's boots, although I only got to do the potato peeling back then. She nodded. 'That would be kind, Tony.'

I never introduced myself properly to Pig Lady, but Rick was always calling out my name: 'T-t-tony.' Back in junior school, I used to have a bit of a stutter, not anymore, but Rick's got a long memory. We grew up in a village just outside Boston, but even we took the piss out of Pig Lady's accent. She was fenlands through and through. Rick used to say, 'They crawled out the mud only a generation back.' Joking of course, but from a quick glance at Pig Lady, you might have thought there was some truth to it. She did have this wet look about her. I don't mean soppy, more like a sheen on her pale skin, a threaded dampness through her short dark hair. I suppose lugging about bins full of food scraps was sweaty work.

Usually it was me who helped her load up with fish skins, potato peelings, batter bits. Rick was on the same youth training scheme as me, but he started a month before, which meant the dirty stuff usually got left to me. I didn't mind so much. Rick was a laugh; everyone knew it. But his brother Gary was a riot.

Gary found the funny side of things every time. When the Saturday girl dropped a bottle of ketchup once, it splattered all up her bare legs. Gary said she'd come on the rag, right there. He cracked everyone up. I was still on the dishwasher then. It steamed and fogged up the end of the kitchen, and the Saturday girl stayed there for the rest of the day. She must have told the manager because Monday comes round and Gary got such a rollicking.

He got the Saturday girl back though, pushed her into the chiller room but she got in a hit first, whacked him with a kilo tub of margarine. Pig Lady heard the shouts, got the girl out, which ruined the joke a bit. But, God, Rick and Gary were funny.

The Saturday girl didn't come back for any more Saturdays. I got moved up from dishwashing to take Gary's place as a trainee after the manager kicked him out. Rick was pretty good about it. And I kept any thoughts I had about having to do all the dirty jobs to myself.

We were getting ready for the pre-match lunch rush that last Saturday when Rick's brother Gary came in. I didn't know it then, but it wasn't going to be like any other Saturday.

Gary asked for the pensioner special, which was only meant for those over sixty-five. But the manager wasn't about, so Rick got Sue to ring it up on the till. Rick usually got what he wanted with a wink and a smile. I bagged it up.

'Ta, T-t-tony,' Rick said. He left the counter, went to share the chips with Gary.

They stood by the big windows at the front of the shop, hair gel greasing up the glass as they leaned their heads against it. Pig Lady called them a pigeon pair once, and they did look like that – chests puffed up, feathered hair at the back of their necks, dark dark eyes. They pointed and laughed at the football crowd stumbling out the pubs, twisting about in the street, trying to remember which way the ground was. They stuck fingers up at OAPs struggling against the wind; mothers bribing away tantrums with Capri Sun and Twix; traders slinging bags of frozen sausages from the back of white vans. Rick and Gary both got sharper when together, like wet haddock dipped in the fryer. Water and oil should never mix. But like Rick and Gary said, it was only a bit of banter.

I kept my hands under the heat lamps, scooping chips and flipping fish when Sue called out each order. I preferred working in the back kitchens. The red and white design of the shop and cafe gave me a headache. But Saturday match days, the manager said everyone had to 'chip in' – Rick coughed, 'Tosser,' under his breath whenever the manager said it. But like I said, the manager wasn't about this last day, so I was stuck on my own at the counter serving-up.

The paper wasn't just wet from steam; some of my sweat got soaked in too. The red striped apron and white waders didn't give much protection. The heat from the fryers behind set my skin on fire, and the blue gloves made the eczema between my fingers crack and bleed.

Rick looked over every now and again, gave Sue a wink and me a nod. He was good like that. Couldn't blame him for larking about, the manager was out after all, and Sue liked a quiet life. Sue told me once about her kids and her boyfriend off on long haulage, said she knew about lads like Rick and Gary, but I never heard her say that to them. The small L shaped burn on her wrist that was leftover from one of Gary's gags – something to do with a heated fry handle and a plastic spider – so many I can't remember them all.

Before Rick got back to filling his face with chips, Gary shouted out, 'Earthquake.'

It wasn't, of course, and that's why it was funny, but this huge woman stepped into the shop. She had to shuffle sideways to fit through the door.

Gary banged the glass, pointing at the red mobility scooter parked on the pavement. 'Bet the suspension on that thing's shot.'

The woman gave this half-smile, half-frown. You could tell she was thinking about going out again, only now an old bloke in a kid's blue mac, straw hat wedged on his head, came in behind her. She had nowhere to go. Had to fit herself into the line as best she could. Rick nudged Gary, and they stared at the stretched seams of her beige leggings.

Gary laughed. 'They should stick a Wide Load sign to that.'

Rick nodded hard as if he'd wanted to say it himself, but things like that would get back to a manger. Some in the queue sniggered, some studied the meal deal chalkboard: onion rings, small chips, soft drink, and fishcake. The huge woman fiddled with the tiny clasp of her heart-shaped purse. More might have been said if the army recruiter hadn't come in for his order of battered sausage, large chips, and mushy peas.

The army still came to Boston's market every couple of months, set up their stall with its colourful posters, and free pens. But there were easier ways to make money was what I thought back then. I flipped fish and scooped chips, watching the football crowds snake down the street.

The army recruiter stepped back against the window to wait for his order.

'Run out of fodder?' Gary said, stuffing another chip in his mouth.

The army recruiter straightened his cuffs, the uniform all edges and angles like it had been carved around him. 'Sign yourself up, lad. Save the Crown some money. Cheaper to train you than let you rot in a cell.'

'The charges didn't stick. I got off,' Gary said. Which was true. The police said there wasn't enough evidence to charge him with assault; the Saturday girl had gone quiet on the chiller room incident, and in the end it was just Gary's word against some crazy fen woman who kept pigs.

The army recruiter smiled. 'That's what we like – lucky lads.'

I laughed, but it couldn't have been a joke because Gary glared as he took bites out of a fish cake. The huge woman in her beige leggings got her order and got away without Gary noticing. He must have been mad about that because he bit the cake in half, nearly taking his finger off too.

The recruiter paid, beckoned me over to the till before he left. He handed over a card: *If you've got it in you, the Army will bring it out.* The paper corners dug into my gloved fingers. 'Think about it,' he said. 'Before you get fried up.'

I didn't know what he was on about then, but I didn't chuck the card away, so maybe I knew it was about to happen. I slipped the hard-edged paper into my shirt pocket before Rick came back behind the counter.

He called out over his shoulder, 'See you later, Gary.'

'See you later, Rick,' Gary answered, making a show of pushing out the shop, stretching his arms above his head, taking up more than his share of space, before marching off down the street.

Rick nudged me out the way of the fryer, lowering a cradle of chipped potatoes into the yellow depths. 'You fetching the swill today, T-t-tony?'

'If you want,' I said.

He only nodded, not having a kid or flicking a wet cloth or anything; I should have known then that something was up. He left the chips to fry, wandered back into the kitchens behind the wall. I expected him to come out with another basin of raw potatoes. Hadn't he just loaded the last of them into the fryer? The chips were going fast. Sue looked up from tapping numbers into the till, counting out change, said, 'Make yourself useful. Bring out more spuds.'

I needed help to fetch the sacks; we'd covered it all in a health and safety session. But the cook and waitresses all made themselves look busy when I asked.

The potato sacks lay in a heap beside the storeroom door. Deliveries were supposed to be put away as soon as they arrived, that was in the training video too, but I knew they'd sit there until the manager got back.

I chose a sack on the outside edge. If I picked the wrong one, the whole lot would topple over. The paper dragged and snagged on the cracked tiles as I pulled it through the steaming corridor. Hard to walk backwards in waders, like slipping around in someone else's skin. The musty smell of earth seeped through the red stitching that kept the sack shut. My arms felt ready to pop out of their joints. Nine trips to go, each bag weighing twenty-five kilos. I wasn't sure how many kilos that was in total but knew it was a lot.

No one liked going to the peeling barrels and chipper. They were kept in a small room at the end of the corridor, at the very rear of the shop, backing right onto the river; down a few steps, sinking below the waterline. The Witham soaked through the bricks and plaster, leaving angry stains that had to be scrubbed away once a week with bleach.

I reached the steps, rested the sack against my shins, shoving the heavy door with my shoulder. But I didn't need to feel for the switch. The light was on. I blinked against its brightness. The potato starch splattered up the walls made the room glow.

In the shadow of the peeling barrels stood Gary and Rick, heads in close, whispering. Gary must have snuck in through a side window because I'd have seen him come back through the shop. The sack shifted against my legs, and I stumbled down a step trying to keep hold of it. It pulled me on. They stared but didn't step forward to help.

Gary picked with his thumbnail at something wedged in his front teeth. Rick ran a hand through his gelled-back hair. They glanced at each other. Gary shifted his head a bit to the left. Rick gave a quick nod. They weren't speaking, but with those movements, I knew they said things to each other.

I got the sack up to the side of the metal tub, propping it, rearranging the weight of potatoes so it didn't tumble over and bruise the white flesh. Without the peelers, banging and scouring off skin, the damp bricks muffled the sounds from the kitchen like a pillow over the head. I turned on the water. Thought it best to get on, pulling back the stitching on the sack, ripping open the paper. The drum began to spin and hum.

Rick picked up the other end of the sack. 'Mates help each other out, don't they?' He looked up at me, but I don't think he wanted an answer. I studied the blur of white flesh and brown water in the peeler.

Gary shrugged, the sports bag on his shoulder slipping off. He yanked it up into place. 'He's a smeghead.'

Rick helped tip the rest of the muddied potatoes into the peeler. He glanced over at his brother, said, 'He's one of us.'

I hadn't noticed Gary's bag when he was in earlier. He gripped the black Slazenger sports kit across his stomach. Rick pushed the button on the peeler. It kicked up a notch; water splashed on my waders. I rushed to push the plastic tray into place so the cleaned spuds didn't bounce off across the concrete floor. They popped out clean as peeled eggs.

Rick grabbed the front of my apron, dragged me over the machine. He held my hand over the blur of metal spikes in the peeling barrel. 'Are you one of us?'

Muddy water splattered up against my chin. I grinned, said, 'You know I am.'

Rick let go. I stood up, scratching at the burning eczema between my fingers.

Gary pulled something from the bag, bounced it in his hands. 'Prove it.'

He threw the thing too fast to tell what it was. It thumped against my chest. I caught it before it slipped to the floor. So cold it burned my hands. 'What is it?'

Gary zipped up the bag. 'It's for a laugh.'

'Gary got it from the school he cleans at,' Rick said.

It was a small creature, a dead one: blue at the tips of the ears, frost on the skin. Snout nose and hooves pearly as fingernails – a piglet. 'What you want me to do with it?'

'Run it through the dishwasher,' Rick said.

'Pink it up,' Gary said. 'Got to look living.'

I weighed it in my hands, wasn't much of a thing, but really I was thinking about my worth. 'Don't need me for that.' I offered up the yellowed body.

Gary lunged for me. Rick grabbed the bag strap, held him back, said, 'What we going to do, Gary? Stick it under the hand dryer?'

Rick hadn't been allowed near the dishwasher since the time he flooded it by not taking the scrunched up paper napkins off the plates. He knew going near it would get back to the manager. Rick grinned. 'Come on, T-t-t... mate.'

Gary picked at the frayed edge of the bag strap but stared at me; felt like I was in the peeling barrel, skin being scrubbed off. Rick elbowed him. Gary sighed, but couldn't stop the grin stretching out his thin lips. 'You are going to piss yourself when this goes down, mate.'

Rick laughed, slapped my arm. 'You in?'

The piglet felt squashed tight, slippery like vacuum-packed cod. I wrapped my apron around it. I nodded. I mean it was only a laugh after all. Didn't everyone laugh at Gary and Rick's jokes? Well, I'd be in on this one.

I didn't know what Gary and Rick wanted the piglet for, but I thought it was going to be one hell of a gag. It was in the dishwasher, going through the cycle. I tried to take my mind off it, but Rick kept flicking peas at me and grinning. Swear, I almost broke two plates and an ice cream sundae glass through holding back the laughter. But I finally got my eye in, putting it all away: glass, mug, knife, plate – a bit like Tetris. The dishwasher was beeping in no time, telling me the load was done.

Rick zigzagged through the kitchen, just missing the swing door opening up from the restaurant, sidestepping the prep station, its stink of sweating butter, and puddles of Marie Rose sauce. He nodded at the dishwasher. I yanked open the door, sliding out the tray. The steam tightened the grins on our faces.

Rick checked over his shoulder, and I did the same. The waitresses came and went behind us, popping out for fags now the lunchtime rush was dying down. The cook microwaved the last of the apple pie: bing, click, chatter, clatter. They didn't know what was coming.

Rick lifted the slippery carcass out of the plate rack, tipped it into a takeaway bag.

'Pig Lady's here,' Sue called as she passed us on her way back to the till. The smell of menthols on her breath was thick as the detergent steam.

It must have been the first time Rick had missed that battered old white van pulling up outside.

'I'll see to it,' I said.

'Nice one.' He slapped my back. 'Hold Pig Lady up for a minute. Got to get everything set, don't want her in the way.'

I met Pig Lady at the door. Sue didn't look up from the till, too busy spearing old receipts. The bell rang as Pig Lady brought the bins inside. She only ever came after the lunchtime rush when the shop was as good as empty. But the marketplace outside was filling up with a post-match crowd; shirt waving, can throwing, they'd be in for their sausage and chips soon.

Pig Lady nodded. 'Done with them waders yet, Tony?'

'Still some tread in them,' I said. 'Been so busy, we haven't brought all the peelings up. Rick won't be long.'

She shifted the bin on her back; dark juice ran down. 'Don't want to make a mess.'

'Hold up, let me get paper towels.' I reached for some off a pile underneath the till, handed them to Pig Lady.

Sue tutted and went back to holding her sleeve up to her nose.

Pig Lady couldn't reach behind herself, handed them back. I dabbed at the stain instead. She stood facing the fridge door, waiting for me to be done, her reflection overlaying the cans of Fanta, Coke, and 7-Up.

Someone banged up against the windows, rushed onwards towards the Three Bells by mates in matching yellow and black club colours. Men drifted against the shop fronts in the marketplace like leaves, filling up the pavement, bumping against each other.

Pig Lady said, 'How's that young Saturday girl?'

Her voice sounded loud in the hush of the shop, all the noise, all the bodies outside the windows, and us inside like we were frozen – maybe that's how the Saturday Girl had felt; I'd not really thought of it like that before.

I got another towel; the muck was bleeding right through the green paper. 'She dropped the charges, I heard.'

Pig Lady shook her head. 'Those brothers are trouble.'

There was blood between my fingers from where I'd scratched the eczema. I rolled off the gloves, dabbed at the blood. 'They're all right.'

'Boy's don't get enough discipline these days. Things would have been different for my John.'

'You got a son?'

She turned, scooped the towels out of my hands. 'Where's Rick got to with those peelings.' She mashed them into her pocket. 'Nothing but the best for my pigs. They'll be hungry.'

I asked, 'Is it true pigs eat each other?'

'Only stillbirths, if you don't get in there quick enough. Three to five per cent of farrowing stillbirths is normal, they say. Don't that seem a lot?'

'Suppose.'

She nodded. 'Seems a lot.'

A policeman stood outside the shop.

'I'll be getting a ticket soon,' Pig Lady said, watching her van. *Patricia Lusby & Son Piggery* was written on the side, the white paint had been picked off *& Son*, but the ghost of it was still there. That's when I remembered something Gary and Rick were laughing about once; about her son's car overturning, trapping him in a deep dyke, and when the police finally found him, days later, he was slippery and wrinkled as a newborn.

'Rick will be right out,' I said, keeping my eyes on the floor.

I don't think we'd ever said so much to each other. She must have felt it too because we didn't say no more as she paced by the front window. Rick should have collected up the peelings ages ago, but I guess the prank was all on his mind. I followed behind her, breathing through my mouth, trying not to taste the stink from the bin on her back.

Rick and Gary came out of the kitchen, pushing past Sue who knew better than to say anything. Rick carried the peelings in a metal barrel.

Pig Lady looked up. 'We should empty that out back. The manager wouldn't like any mess in front.'

Gary had the paper takeaway bag wrapped in his arms, pressed to his chest. I knew what he carried in there, only it didn't seem so funny now that piglet inside was pinked and hot from the dishwasher, newborn.

'We're here now,' Rick said, nudging Gary, holding back a snort.

I reached for Pig Lady's bin. 'I'll do it out back.'

Rick stopped me, his hand on my chest. 'You're not going nowhere.' He said something else, but I couldn't hear it even as his voice got louder trying to compete with the growing noise in the street. I just wanted the joke to be over. The window shook as someone banged up against it again. Pig Lady stepped towards it, put her hand on the glass. A crowd swelled in the marketplace. Against the plate glass window of the chip shop, a group of men had the policeman pinned.

Gary banged back on the glass. 'They got a pig.'

Rick banged too, snorting loudly.

Pig Lady dropped her bin, walked out into the shop's entranceway, knocking against the backs of the crowd. I watched through the window. She pushed her way between them, waving her arm in front of her as if she was seeing off crows.

Gary laughed. 'Hope they don't do her too badly, we've still got some fun lined up.'

Rick leaned against the window, mimed licking the back of the policeman's head. The man's helmet was knocked to the ground, disappearing under boots and trainers. The crowd pulsed forward. Pig Lady's dark hair disappeared for a moment then bobbed to the surface near the front. She stood in front of the policeman. Punches landed between the windmill of her arms. No one else was attempting to help. I squeezed the lip of the bin she'd left behind; knuckles white. Couldn't move.

Pig Lady didn't shout, didn't hit out. She stood still: a barrier. Shamed by that referee acting as the mob's conscience, the crowd began to break up into men again; arms and legs separating, individuals emerging from the hissing mass. The losing team drifted off, red football scarves trailing in puddles. Pig Lady helped the policeman up, handed him his helmet. He shook her hand, turned away to speak into a radio. Pig Lady came back to the shop.

Sue said to her, 'What did you do that for? Could have got yourself hurt.'

Why did Pig Lady stand in front of that crowd? How did she know what to do? I wouldn't know what to do.

She eased the bin from my hands. 'Some fights you have to take on, even if you think you might lose. Now, let's get this done,' she said.

Gary nodded. 'Sure thing.' He reached for the wrapped-up piglet.

And I never asked Gary and Rick what the joke was, how they were going to make a defrosted piglet funny – that pink, soft body – where was the fun in that?

They stepped towards Pig Lady. She just stood, watched, didn't know what was coming either. I picked up the metal barrel of peeling scraps, wanted to get this done, to get her gone. Gary reached into the paper bag. Rick nudged him in the ribs.

Gary winked at Sue. 'Here, watch this.'

Whatever it was, it was going to be now. But I didn't want to see any more of their jokes; not a pinked-up piglet and her not knowing what was coming; her son and those days of waiting as he lay sunk in the watery dyke; Gary and Rick just waiting to laugh at all that pain. I lifted the cold metal barrel off the ground. Usually it weighed so much more. Pig Lady waited with her hands around the empty black bin. Rick and Gary getting closer. They pushed past. What could I do? Do something. I lifted the barrel higher, spun about.

I tipped the peelings barrel over Gary, dropped it down on his head. He sank to his knees. Muddy peelings, fish skins, bones sliding out over the floor, splattering all over Rick too. He squealed, jumped back.

'Just a joke,' I said.

No one laughed. There was only us, silence, the potato peelings, and the stink of the River Witham, all soaking into the bricks and plaster of the old fish and chip shop. The brown stain of food waste oozing up against the wall. I kicked the paper bag out from the heap, reached inside and took out the piglet carcass. Slipped it, warm and soft, into the front pocket of my apron. Walked out of the shop. The tinkle of the bell was the last thing I remember, before finding myself at the back of Nan's flat, mud on my hands, smoothing the earth under her roses hard and flat. There were much worse places that piglet could have ended up.

Pig Lady went on with her rounds, collecting slop for the hungry pigs, no real harm done. The policeman would have been fine by next match day, I'm sure of it. I bet Gary and Rick are still up to their tricks – what a pair! That's probably what happened. I can't say for sure. I signed up for the Royal Anglian Regiment soon as I could. Haven't been back to Boston, haven't been back to the chip shop.

I've done all the training, catering corps. Now I'm waiting for a first tour of duty. Waiting for the thunder of live rounds outside the mess tent, the blast of bombs echoing over the desert, to make me feel brave. Waiting. Only I don't hold out much hope. I'll never really be brave, not like what I saw that last Saturday at the chip shop, saw in Patricia Lusby. But I'll be there all the same, offering support to those that can. It's little more than anyone would have ever expected of me, but it's so much more than I ever expected of myself.

Zoom

It starts in darkness. Then the interior light comes on.

A boy sits in the front passenger seat. He twists round to say something to a younger boy in the back. It zooms in closer. The car is gone, just two faces at the window. The younger boy is wearing Spiderman pyjamas. The zoom wobbles; it makes the boys look like they are shaking. The older boy faces forward again. Why doesn't he see it coming?

You have been filming them for two weeks. The school assignment was called Getting to Know Your Neighbours. You were supposed to interview them, but the farm on the left was empty; even the for sale sign was broken. And the neighbours on the right: Mrs Phipps and the boys had moved out, ten miles away to Boston, last summer; Mr Phipps was always working in the fields that surrounded the house. So, you took to filming them instead like one of those Attenborough programmes your dad watched on box sets.

This is the third time of watching. The zoom is good enough to show the younger boy playing with the straps of his car seat. He looks nearly big enough to use a grown-up belt, but he won't ever get that chance. The clip plays on a loop.

Nothing much happened until last weekend. Mrs Phipps had dropped the boys at the gate; she never went up to the house anymore. The boys got half-way down before they saw it. The black bull was out, wedged under the hedge like a huge meteor fallen to earth. Mr Phipps shouting from the house. Mrs Phipps scream-

ing from her car. The bull lifted its heavy head, breaking apart the hawthorn. You filmed it all from your bedroom window.

Mrs Phipps won. The boys ran back to her; they drove off and didn't stay for their weekend visit. The car was a safe place that day.

Here comes the next bit already.

The mike isn't good enough to pick up sound, but the man outside the car must be speaking. The older boy, the one in front, reaches down to undo his belt. He leans to the right, flicking the car headlights on. The zoom lurches up. It's Mr Phipps standing there. The fenland slips into grey, a purple glow surrounding Boston Stump like a bruise. It drops back to the car. The younger boy yawns, scratching at the neck of his Spiderman pyjamas. Why aren't they in bed?

That morning, Mr Phipps had a delivery of sheep. Something to record at last. You took Sammy to see them in the field opposite. Keep that dog away from my stock, Mr Phipps said. But Sammy was always on a lead, not like the Alsatian from the weekend cottages down the road. Twelve years old, tall for your age, but his snout reached your stomach. That dog chased you whenever you rode your bike past, snapping and snarling, and always barked when Mr Phipps fired cartridge-scarers up into the sky.

You went back to the gate, filming from behind a telephone pole; zooming in. Mr Phipps talking to your dad about the sheep like they were his babies, all soft and cooing: how the price of lamb was on the up, how he was going to make a killing. Do up the farm and get them all back on their feet, get back his wife and his boys.

Mr Phipps said things were going to happen. Mr Phipps said he was sure of it.

It stays with the two boys, in profile, like a shot from *You've Been Framed*: waiting for a monkey to steal a windscreen wiper, for someone to jump out wearing a monster mask. But none of those things are going to happen. No laughter track, no music, no voiceover, no caption – footage contains some images that viewers may find disturbing. It is going to happen. It will happen soon.

It zooms out. Mr Phipps is moving around the car, bending down then bobbing up again further away in the field. The younger boy's head drops forward. He is asleep. The older boy in front leans his chin on the dashboard, tracing his finger across the windscreen. He must be cold, or he is playing make-believe, because he lifts the hood of his Nike sweater over his head. His face becomes a black hole.

It was the night of the predicted meteor shower. You had set your alarm for 11.30 p.m., in case you fell asleep; practising the shot through the bedroom window. A new man, Mrs Phipps' boyfriend, had dropped the boys off for their weekend visit. But nothing else happened, and you waited for it to get dark. Lights were on at the holiday cottage; someone calling for the Alsatian. It barked, off in the distance. The wind came off the Wash, sweeping the clouds away towards the Midlands. A clear view straight up into the sky. No trees or hills to break the flat farmland that stretched and stretched.

Still the interior light and the two boys: one sleeping, one running his fingers, like short pumping legs, along the dash. The older boy checks the car clock; the time can't be seen from this angle. The zoom moves again. He sets to drumming, glancing over his shoulder. The younger boy sleeps on, hands jerking; he must be dreaming. Neither boy gets up to see what is happening outside the car. Would things be different if they did?

You had zoomed in and out, getting the focus right. Your dad hadn't even noticed his smartphone was missing. Your sister already asleep in the bed furthest from the door, the nightlight shining on her face. You turned away from the window and zoomed in on your sister: mouth gulping, eyelashes fluttering. You took it even closer into a blur of pink and red flesh. The zoom was strong enough to record the whole thing.

Mr Phipps appears again, this time at the back of the car. The older boy looks up. The boot opens and shuts. The face is gone. Things look different at night. The boy slides over to the driver's seat and waves. He opens the door, facing away from the camera now. His padded coat looks like a harlequin print, but that is only the light. He sits back; the coat becomes navy blue again.

You noticed that everything looked different at night, dipped in blue: the hawthorn bush next door like a giant bony hand, fingers spread open in defence; the RAF landing lights at the end of the field like red Chinese lanterns blown off course. The sheep were stone still, illuminated by moonlight; no streetlamps that far out of the village. You had thought then that the sheep must be sleeping deeply like your sister, but it turned out that you were wrong.

It shows the older boy putting one hand on the wheel as if he is driving it. He steers carefully, and he should have made a good driver. His hand imagines the move of changing gears, or at least his shoulder, visible through the window, echoes this movement. The hood slips down a little. Dark, close-cut hair grows low on his forehead or perhaps he is frowning.

Soon the meteor would pass close enough to shatter into a thousand or more shooting stars over earth. You started recording.

Lights moved over Mr Phipps' field, the one in front of the house. The Alsatian was barking; running away from the sheep field, along the top of the dyke. Maybe it had started early. But it was only a car turning off the road and onto the track. Headlights bumping along, but it was too dark to see who was inside. The car stopped.

Then the interior light came on.

The older boy slips his hands inside his pockets. It is getting cold. He yawns and checks the clock again. He is the sensible one; he knows it is past their bedtime. The zoom catches Mr Phipps outside the car. It looks like he is carrying a stick; lifting it up to point at something in the dark.

The zoom follows him back to the car. The older boy sits up straight.

That small movement is familiar: the nod as the boy returns to the passenger seat for the final time. How many times has it been now?

It was still playing; loop after loop. The zoom had been strong enough to record the whole thing. But this time you didn't want to see it alone. Clouds blacked out the moon; there would be no meteor shower tonight. You moved away from the window; needed to share it, to have someone else watch it too. To make sure it was realer than one of those nightmares where your legs turned to stone and your mouth filled with cotton wool, or one of those horror films where the action slowed and the camera entered with the bullet.

It will happen soon: the older boy in front, the younger boy asleep in the red and black car seat; Mr Phipps pushing his head so it is just inside the door.

The light shows Mr Phipps and his boys.

You ran across the room, landing with a thud on the Peppa Pig duvet set. Your sister turned over, grunting, burying her face in the pillow. You grabbed her shoulders, shook her awake. Pulled her up into a sitting position; shaking again until her eyes rolled open.

This is it.

Mr Phipps holds up the thick, black stick, but it isn't a stick. The shotgun flashes. The boy slumps back against the passenger door, glass shatters into a thousand cubes of light. The zoom shakes as if it feels the ricochet. The hood slips back from what is left of the boy's face. Blood stains the windscreen black.

The younger brother wakes. He scratches at the seat straps trapping him, just as he did in sleep. But now his eyes are open. The shot kills him before he opens his mouth. His arms and legs fly up and fall back as if the car has been hit from behind by an articulated lorry. The straps keep his body in place. He doesn't slide out of view like his older brother has.

The interior light goes off, but it doesn't end yet. There is a third flash. The zoom doesn't shake this last time. It settles on the dead sheep scattered in the field, throats torn out.

That's not real, your sister said. Did you get it off the net? she said. Is it top-ranked on YouTube? she said. You tell your sister you found it. Where? she said. You pointed to the window. All the sound in the world came back

now. So loud even Mrs Phipps, ten miles away in Boston, must be able to hear.

Your sister screams and screams; screams and screams.

Dinner Dance

In Whitechapel, London, there stands a pub where you can eat a kebab and watch a woman strip. It isn't in the guidebooks.

Push open the frosted-glass door and head towards the red hatch on the left. Place an order and choose between chilli or garlic sauce. Next stop, the bar. Tap only, no bottles here. Don't squeeze the pint too hard, brittle plastic cracks, and beer collects like teardrops on fingers.

Fluorescent lights wipe out shadows except dark circles under eyes. The evening drinkers and Jack the Ripper sightseers are gone, only the midnight crowd gather. They stand in small groups like leaves blown in off the street. The square wooden planks of the stage rise up and pen them in. Nobody moves; hands grip pitta as iceberg lettuce melts into the floor.

A man in blue Reebok tracksuit bottoms tugs on a suit jacket and shoulders his way to the front. He holds an old jam jar, and greasy fingers drop in pound coins; click and rattle. Have the cash ready, no UB40, senior, or student discounts; don't ask for change. Only when the glass is packed with gold, do the lights blink off. The red curtain twitches; music thrums from a ghetto blaster on the bar. A woman strides onto the stage. She adjusts a bra-strap with the twitch of black painted nails.

Ignore the stretch marks on her thighs and breasts: it is the yellow lamps at the corner of the stage that make the valleys run deep. She is barely eighteen for those who wish hard enough. Her spine twists as the music vibrates through her steady legs. Eyes fixed on the cracked tiles of the mirrorball; nostrils flared against the cold metallic smell of garlic in the air. She pivots, tilts backwards towards the floor, cantilevers with her right foot; hands tweaking the frayed cords that tie her bra and knickers into place.

A fourth cover version is playing before she stands naked. The song keeps beating, but she is done. She turns to the curtain and bows, stiffly from the waist, to pick up the thong; her lips hairless as the doner pirouetting on its pole. Sweat dribbles. No one reaches out to touch; they bite into bread and meat and take another gulp of London Pride.

The lights come up. Faded red velvet sweeps the stage, and she vanishes – until the jar is full again.

Freshwater

The second time our mother left, we packed the car with deflated beach balls, rolled up lilos, towels, and booze. Dad drove us to Freshwater. The clapperboard chalet had belonged to our maternal grandmother. A signboard tilted out onto the pavement: *For Sale*. And that's when we knew our mother wasn't coming back.

By the time we unloaded, the sun was setting behind the reeds at the back of the garden. We sat on the concrete patio, yellowing plastic chairs creaking, watching the horizon burn. There were four of us kids: Aaron the oldest at nineteen; us middle ones, Ben and Carrie, at eighteen and sixteen; and Diane the youngest at thirteen. We held out the blue plastic beakers; Dad topped them up with gin. There wasn't any ice. A carton of Marlboro Reds lay open on the table.

We smoked and we drank.

The beakers were warm and sticky in our hands, but a breeze wormed its way up from the baked mud of the riverbed, wriggling through the humid July evening. The gin tasted sharp like tears.

We didn't talk much; we drank more.

Ben dug out an old board game from a cupboard in the living room. *Game of Life*. It was bowed with water damage, but we picked up the plastic car counters anyway, forcing them uphill at times, sticking in pin people, working our way through the game. We played until the light failed us.

A bulb hanging in the kitchen behind us wasn't bright enough to hold back darkness, swallowing up even the outline of our toes. Pheasants cried for their mates, stalking the reeds at the edge of the grass. No stars, but the moon appeared from the clouds every now and again, bringing the molehills, the cracked angles of the plastic chairs, into focus. The green glow of Dad's Casio watch pulsed, beeping to some timetable we didn't know about.

Time stretched around the chalet. Peeling white paint, small leaded windows like a cricket hut from one of those Sunday night dramas our mother used to watch. Diane began to hum the *Miss Marple* theme music, dropping notes until it was tuneless as the buzz of gnats about our ears. Ben threw a packet of fags at her. She reached in, stuck a cigarette between her lips. The blue lighter lay on the patio table beside the abandoned game. Dad was nearest to it. Diane eased herself up, kneeling in the grass, stretching for the lighter. No one stopped her.

Five red tips glowed in the grey gloom. Gnats feasted on us. No one swatted them away.

Dad was the first to leave the garden, calling from the doorway, 'See you in the morning.' But his voice rose at the end as though it was a question he wanted to ask.

Us kids took the bedroom; a double, and a single with another mattress that slid out from underneath. Candlewick bedspreads in shades of pink and green lay across our feet, and we sweated through the winceyette sheets. Our mother must have slept in the same bed when she was a girl, younger than Diane now. She was an only child; maybe back then she longed for company. She used to tell us about this place, but somehow we'd never got round to visiting.

The ceiling sloped towards our heads. The blue-flowered wallpaper felt hairy, damp like an old flannel. It was a bit like camping.

Dad slept on a lilo pressed against the wall in the lounge; no settee, only those wingback chairs old folks have. We heard the squelch of the plastic all night. He turned and turned, turned and turned.

The next morning, we found Dad on the floor, the sheets twisted about his legs. The lilo gave one last dying gasp as he sat up, opened a can of Heineken. We followed ants marching down the corridor, stepping over them to get to the kitchen. Sand under the orange lino crackled, making us notice the itchy gnat bites on our arms and legs. We scratched, shedding ashy flakes of skin.

No one remembered to bring milk, so we had cornflakes with water, and a couple of beers each for breakfast. We carried the rest of the beers, the lilos, beach balls, and some towels, through the gravel car park, across the road, and over the sea-wall to Freshwater beach.

'I don't need any help,' Dad shouted.

He blew up two lilos and two rainbow-coloured beach balls. We lay on the towels waiting for him to be done. Diane burned cigarettes into the plastic castle-shaped bucket. There wasn't any sand on the beach, only smooth pebbles that felt like Murray Mints when grasped in your hand.

Dad slapped the lilos on the water; spray splashed over his rolled-up jeans and bare chest. We hobbled over the shingle to the shoreline, except Aaron who didn't want to leave his can of beer. Despite the heat of the day, the water nipped at our ankles. Dad steadied the red lilo with his hands. Us girls struggled on, slipping against the hard plastic. It made farting noises as we tried to find a balance, its ridged and wrinkled edges scratching our legs.

Ben tried to clamber on next.

'You're too big,' Dad said.

Ben stood belly-deep in the water, arms over his chest, watching us get hauled away. He sat astride the other lilo, but the waves kept pushing him back towards shore. He dragged the yellow lilo up the beach, weighed it down with pebbles and beach towels. The wind was too strong for the beach balls. They rolled away, disappearing over the seawall, off to find some other kid in some other place.

Dad dragged us girls through the waves. We laughed and screamed until holidaymakers tutted and shook their heads. We shouted louder after that. He ran parallel with the beach, twisting, then pushing us out to sea. Our legs, hanging over the sides, grew numb. Behind us, life on the beach shrank smaller and smaller. Dad's chin dipped under the level of the waves. If he let go, slipped and sank out of sight, would anyone notice? How far would we drift?

Diane began to rock, pitching forward. She puked; swallowing too much seawater will do that to you. It frothed like lager, running between the plastic grooves. We wriggled, ready to abandon ship.

'It's too deep. Stay on,' Dad said.

He half-swam, half-dragged us through the cold water. We reached the shallows. Dad collapsed on top of the red plastic. We rolled off, banging our knees on the shelf of pebbles. Waves buffeted him, but the inflatable held him up. We staggered out of the sea, shivering; watched him from further up the beach. Hunched, raw from the sun and the salt, he looked like a deflating beach ball.

'Want a beer, Dad?' Aaron called.

Dad waved a limp hand, signalling he'd be right back. Aaron screwed the spare can into the stones, shielding it from the sun. The pebbles were stacked on top of each other, crevices and holes all around. We dropped cigarette butts, ring pulls, straws. It was possible to lose so many things between the cracks.

'I'm hungry,' Diane said. She sat herself on my outstretched legs, which took us both by surprise. I opened my knees, and she dropped down onto the beach, bum shuffling away. She wrapped herself tighter in the towel. Against the backdrop of the sea, she looked so small.

Other families went to the tearooms, the chip shop, or unwrapped clingfilm cosseted sandwiches, unscrewed tartan flasks of steaming tea when lunchtime came. We drank the rest of the beer, smoked a packet of cigarettes, chewed our nails. The sun overhead so bright that it ate up its own shadow.

After lunch, the tide came in, pushing the beachgoers closer together, jostling with their chairs and windbreakers. Dad lay in the sun, eyes hidden behind a pair of plastic Mickey Mouse sunglasses he'd found on the promenade; the small arms stretched to snapping point. Mums applied sun lotion; fathers read newspapers; pensioners sucked on Mr Whippy soft-serve; kids paddled. The slick, the rustle, the slurp, the splash. The sweet and salty smell of the seaside crowded about us.

The steps under the corner of the seawall were empty. We went there instead. Dad couldn't be moved.

Waves bashed against the top, feathering us with foam. We took it in turns to launch ourselves onto the lilo, cresting the surf, getting washed back onto the steps.

A man with a Labrador, up on the promenade, said, 'Shouldn't be jumping off there. You kids will do yourself some damage.'

Ben laughed, took another dive.

The square-edged bruise on his thigh lingered for weeks, dark and angry.

The next day even the cornflake packet sat empty. We went to the Spar.

The shop smelled of iced buns and the vents over the aisles puffed out hot breath. Every corner of the ceiling had a security mirror, distorting us as though we were walking through a fairground hall of mirrors. We shared the last of the Heineken, passing the can from hand to hand until it was warm as tea. We picked up a cauliflower and a sachet of cheese sauce, chucked it in the basket. The powder inside the packet was set like concrete. When we add water to it later (because we'll forget the milk again) it won't turn out much better. The rest of the basket was taken up with beer, a bottle of own-brand vodka, and a loaf of Mother's Pride. From the running total Ben kept calling out, we were twenty pence away from nothing when we reached the counter.

The old woman on the till rang up the food, but her hand hovered over the booze. She twisted the gold rings on her swollen fingers. Ben put the tenner on the counter.

The woman said, 'I haven't got change. Maybe you should come back later with your parents.'

Aaron picked a postcard from the wire rack. A handwritten sticker poked out the top: *20 pence each*. 'No need for change,' he said.

The woman pushed her glasses high up on her nose, peered at each of us. 'I believe you're going to supply alcohol to a minor.'

Aaron shrugged. 'There's nothing you can do about it. Believe.'

The wrinkle faced woman didn't offer us a bag, and we didn't ask; cradling the stuff in our arms. We walked through the car park, stopping outside The Anchor to collect Dad. An old bloke, in a black suit and white vest, sat opposite him on the picnic bench. A dried yellow stain on his lapel was shaped like a boot. He smiled at Diane, 'What you got there, missy?'

She held out the postcard. A banner across the middle read, *Seven Wonders of the Isle of Wight*.

Diane read them out. 'Ryde where you can walk. Cowes you can't milk—'

Dad flicked the back of the card. 'Who you sending it to?'

Diane shrugged. She put the postcard on the bench as if it weighed too much to hold.

Dad slammed down his pint glass. 'You kids know where your mother is?'

We shook our heads.

The old bloke leaned across, tapped a square picture. 'This place is one of them wonders. "Freshwater you can't drink".' The same rocky outcrop and pebble beach could be seen if you looked over the road. 'But they got it wrong,' he said. 'Freshwater bubbles up through the salt. Brings good luck to those that see it. Looks like smoke out in those rock pools. Cools the air like ice cubes dropped in a drink. It's a wonder all right.'

We left the shopping with Dad, ran all the way.

Skidding over the seaweed-covered rocks. Other kids looked up from their beach fun, heads turning to watch us fly by. We held out our arms, lending each other balance. Someone laughed, and we bounced that sound between us.

The pools were clustered under the chalk rock-face at the far end of the beach. The tide eased itself out leaving pools exposed, ringed with emerald weeds and bristling red anemones. We crouched around the deepest one.

We waited for the smoky mist to show us that fresh water was coming. We waited for the sweet scent of it. Maybe salt would harden on the drying rocks, pushed out by the springing of fresh water. Maybe sunlight reflecting off those crystals would dazzle birds in the sky. We waited, knees aching, jagged edges of the rocks biting into our pumps.

We waited.

Diane was the first to leave, and somehow with her gone, there was no need for us older ones to stay. We all walked away; perhaps things would have been different if we had turned to look at each other, seen our own pain staring back. I suppose we'll never really know.

That holiday was over twenty years ago. The last time we were together. Diane and Dad stay in touch sometimes; the boys not so much. Being all together would only make it easier to see what was missing. The chalet must have sold; our mother must have kept the cash – can't blame her for that. We've never been back, but I believe we're all still there: standing on the rocks, staring into the pool, waiting for fresh water that will never spring.

Human Terrain

A latecomer slides into the middle row.

'War Studies?' he asks the brunette next to him. She nods.

I tell the students to put away their texts. 'History isn't in those books,' I say.

'Where is it then?' the latecomer asks.

A girl in the front runs a finger over her iPhone. 'Bomb in Pakistan kills twelve. Syria accused of chemical attack. It's in the news,' she says.

I shake my head. 'News can often be as close to a fairy tale as Cinderella. As researchers, students, our job is to read between—'

'What about primary sources?' the latecomer says.

They all want something to hold up and say, Here it is: the truth. I only have these slides to show them. I press the button. *Click.* The projector beam snares dust, splitting apart rainbow colours before it hits the whiteboard.

'Here is one truth,' I say. 'On Monday the fifth of March 2007, a car bomb exploded in Mutanabi Street, Iraq's Green Zone in Baghdad's bookselling quarter. Thirty people were killed. The fragments you'll see here today were found scattered in the rubble, collected and preserved.' If my voice shakes when I say that date, no one in the room notices.

'Slide one,' I say. 'A page from a girl's diary, age eleven and three quarters...'

'But it's in English,' the latecomer says.

'A translation isn't a primary source at all,' says the brunette next to him.

'Translated and interpreted through the eyes of an adult but maintaining the child's narrative of her world at one particular moment,' I say.

'Why do we need to know about some girl and her family?' he says.

'At the bottom is a bit about their Honda being stolen. Maybe this is to do with the car bomb,' the girl with the iPhone says.

'My brothers are serving in Iraq,' says the red-haired boy in the third row.

Some families circulate the armed forces in their blood as if they have a red poppy rooted in their hearts. My daughter wasn't from such a family, but that didn't stop her swearing to defend and honour.

Hana was there that day. Clean-up operations. She collected floating pages from between the rubble, kept them with her kit. It must have been for a reason, a story to tell? But she never really was one for stories; when she was little, I tried to read her the great myths and epic tales. She was always asleep before I finished a page. But she would have made a good historian, questioning everything – Why, Mum? Who says it happened that way? What happens to us when we die?

Click.

'Slide two. Probably a medical textbook. Note the words: "luminal obstruction, ineffective venous and lymphatic drainage. Bacterial invasion ultimately leading to..."'

'*Deeaaaath*,' the latecomer mimes a pantomime choking scene.

Laughter thumps against the peeling green paint on the walls. I lean against the lectern, let it take some of the weight. The water in the glass is dusty, left over from another class, but I drink it anyway. It sticks like grit between my teeth. Our first beach holiday to the Isle of Wight, Hana refused to eat any sandwiches because of the sand. But as an Arabic speaker, she must have known where they would send her. Some of the students are tapping at keyboards, and the more they take notes, the more they raise their hands, the more I feel it all slipping away like sand through my fingers. But these fragments of paper, a manual, a schoolgirl's diary – they are something Hana touched, important enough to keep tucked between her spare socks and chocolate stash.

'I signed up for War Studies, not show and tell,' the latecomer grins.

Hana's mouth was smart too, even as a child she was full of backchat. But that Monday satellite call, our last, was pitted with silences. She said the connection was bad, but it wasn't that. I wondered afterwards if that space on the line was a sign of the final silence that was waiting for us.

'Is the historian only there to cut the flesh, deliver the evidence? Or are they there at inception, sweating, thrusting, creating life? Can we trust our sources?'

Click.

'"What you seek you shall not find,"' reads the girl with the iPhone. 'It's shorter than a tweet.'

'That's a poem, *Gilgamesh*. We did it last term,' says the brunette.

'A voice captured in time, preserved down the ages,' I say.

The latecomer yawns, stretches his arms behind his head. 'None of this stuff is real,' he says.

'If I hadn't made fresh copies of these papers but left the dust and the blood, maybe they would be more real, even if the Arabic couldn't be understood?'

But he isn't listening to me. He passes a Post-it note to the brunette; it sticks to his thumb before he shakes it off. I wanted something of Hana's to stick to me. When I cleared out her room, I hoped to uncover a diary, dig up forgotten letters – anything to hear her voice in my head again. But there was only dust under the bed, desiccated moths at the back of the cupboard. When her box of possessions wrapped in airmail tape arrived, those scraps of paper fell out like dried petals. I tried to put them together like the wooden jigsaw puzzles we did when she was small – translating them into English, as if I could make the words fit together better that way.

'The module description said this class was about conflicts, not this stuff,' the latecomer says.

I open my mouth to answer, but my tongue feels too big, as if it might flop onto the lectern for all to see. That is how it's felt since it happened; each day I carry Hana not in me but on the outside like an open wound.

'Human terrain. The Army acknowledges, through the lessons of Afghanistan and Iraq, that human geography is as important as any satellite map.'

'Can we have a definition for the exam?' the latecomer asks.

I see them watching me like I'm just a slide projection, the captured image of a relic in a museum display case. I don't answer his question. A few inch their textbooks closer, others stare at the whiteboard beside me; I know all about that sweep-over look. Grief corrodes and poisons like a chemical attack. A friend from yoga abandoned her trolley in the freezer aisle of Waitrose just to avoid brushing past me; the kettle is always free when I enter the staff room; my diary cleared before the condolence cards hit the mat.

'Let me show you an example from an unidentified source.'
Click.

I give them time to process the words, from a poem or a prayer. It tells of clouds between rooftops, sky turning red, a desert storm fighting to break over the city walls, of starlings that are the first to return after the dust and the smoke and the screams have gone.

The sniggering has stopped.

'Al Mutanabi was a great Iraqi poet, the bookselling quarter a place of ideas and words and learning. What message would destroying such a place send?'

'Proust said it well enough: "the past made arid by intellect",' the latecomer says. 'Maybe someone wanted to start a new order.'

'Or control that intellect,' says the girl on the right, styrofoam cup nestled between her palms.

I assess the human terrain of the room: they look so young; jaws yet to gain angles, eyes yet to cloud. The brunette has moved her arm closer to the latecomer; now they are touching. She writes something on the Post-it, slides it back to him. He will probably buy her a drink after class; she will buy the next round; tomorrow neither of them will wake up alone.

If I had known how my story would unfold, I would never have used contraception. I should have stacked up children like a survivalist hordes tinned goods. But it wouldn't have made what happened any less painful. Just like Hana's satellite calls that I looked forward to so much always left me with an ache deep in my gut, the final click of the receiver like a raw papercut.

The brunette taps a Biro against her teeth: click click. Head on one hand, tilting her view of the room. They think I'm only some old woman; my class only pass or fail. But I'm not done with them yet.

'The final slide,' I say, 'is a photograph of the city. Shutters are up along Mutanabi Street, blue groundsheets loaded with books and printer cartridges. Not worrying about the cars parked so close to the shop fronts, not worrying about her next call of duty, not worrying about anything but the fresh white pages of precisely the one perfect book she just has to buy, my daughter writes herself into our history lesson.'

'Your daughter?' The brunette drops her pen; it rolls towards the front.

'Hana collected up the floating pages she found that day…'

'What about the car bomb?' the latecomer says.

So he was listening after all. But I don't tell them how those papers were shipped back to me, along with her coffin swaddled in a flag. I mounted the scraps between cellophane sheets at the dining table, shrinking them onto slides as the grief expanded around me. But what did I hope to convey? To teach something of war? Of love?

The iPhone on the front desk vibrates, pulling them away from the picture of Baghdad. Time up.

'She wasn't killed by the car bomb,' I say.

They smile, exhale a breath. I turn off the projector as they make for the exit. The door shuts behind them. Click.

It was sniper fire that killed her, later that night. Up on a hill (I don't know its name), an insurgent took aim (I don't know his name). At the occupiers, the destroyers, the infidels. A trigger clicked, a bullet travelled – ripping through Hana's oesophagus, ricocheting off Hana's spine, lodging in Hana's heart. My future ripped apart by another man's past.

History it isn't.

We Want It Out

You see, the problem isn't that the car is in the swimming pool; the problem is that the neighbours want it out. 'It's a fire hazard, Lynn,' they said. 'It could go up like... well, like a car bomb, Lynn,' they said. I wasn't even aware they knew my name, but apparently a car in the pool is better than an acronym as an aid to remembering.

It's been down there a week; parked under the water.

I sit and drink my coffee. An oily rainbow from the turning goat's milk mirrors the glaze of petrol on the water. It's my daughter who buys the stuff, insisting on organic. 'All other dairy is loaded with carcinogens,' she tells me. When she comes over, I pretend my coffee is that chicory stuff as she has lots to say about caffeine too. I haven't the heart to tell her, 'Really, love, it's a bit late for all that.'

I wonder how long it would take to corrode away? Probably more than a lifetime, but maybe if I leave it long enough, it will be someone else's problem.

The dragonflies are early this year, dipping and kissing the water's edge. I loved those yellow tiles when I first had them laid, but now they remind me of the scrubbed, yellow lino of Riverside Walk at Lewisham Hospital. The corridor snakes, always taking me too quickly to the hushed sigh of those automatic doors. Last week the shopping trolleys and mallard ducks outside the ward window were joined by an up-turned Mini Metro. 'Joyriders,' the nurse said as she hooked me up. Drip after drip the chemicals were fed into me.

Those drips were small as the red bubbles rising from the car now. I stare into the pool; it can't be rust, too soon for that. I prod one with my finger. It doesn't burst but surfaces a few millimetres away – just out of reach. Must be the brake fluid, which is funny because I didn't use them. I floated, me and the car, for what seemed like hours before we sank. The bursting of the fence, tearing up of grass, was joyful loud like a colliery band. But the water was cold as the gel pads the nurse fitted to my hands and head during treatment. 'The drugs are boiling you up,' she said, 'we need to keep you cool.' Not that it made any difference as I watched clumps of my hair float away from my head. I fish a grey strand out of the water.

It was beautiful that day; too sunny and warm for spring. The car windows down so I could feel the wind, feel something. I suppose I wanted to tear it all up, the fence, the grass, the pool. Everything. The day should have been cold, wet, an angry storm setting in. But the rush of air, the chill smack of the water, the ridiculousness of it all, made me slap my hand over my mouth, keeping the laughter inside and the water out.

My daughter came over when she heard. Her arms loaded with printouts from the internet – all about battles, survivors, fighters – making it sound like I had a choice. I wasn't trying to kill myself, not with the car, nor the coffee, the salt, the processed food, the sugar. Sometimes things just happen.

I dunk another chocolate Hobnob. The grey hair floats away just as easily as I did. The car windows open, the lift of the water, click of the seatbelt, slipping up and away.

I'm still here, drinking my coffee, enjoying a biscuit, feeling the sun on my face, so let them have what they want – we all want it out.

I make the call. I sit and wait.

Now the men with their cranes and yellow fluorescent jackets are here; walking through the hole in my fence like this is common land. The doctors in their fluorescing white coats did the same when they lifted my arm above my head, prodded their icy fingers into my breast; holding up X-rays of my lungs, half-moon shaped like the pool. 'You see,' they said, pointing out dark shadows. 'The problem isn't that the cancer is there, the problem is that we can't get it out.'

Things We Did When We Were Children

We didn't go to school that day. We packed a suitcase and a handbag each.

On the plane, we glanced at each other. Smiling. We thought there was nothing to stop us, nothing but blue sky all around. One of us, switching her mobile to flight mode, remembered her family at home, back in that city down below. Thinking this was for the best, to up and leave with no notice. Some of us left letters, scrawled in blue ink with hearts filling the bottom of the page, but others of us left nothing behind. Nothing but everything we had known: our rooms, our duvets, our books, our posters on the wall. We had no need for kids' things. All that's behind us, we said to each other. But we didn't know that some of us would never go to sleep again without remembering that little pink-painted bedroom and the warmth of our mother's skin.

Some of us took our time in the small plane toilet, feeling the trickle of water from the tap, wondering if any tears would be shed for us. Some of us enjoyed the closeness of the seats, of our Sisters beside us. Some of us knew only the presence of others, the heat of breath, the musk of deodorant and sweat, and we had no idea what it was to be alone. Some of us grew up in houses large enough to never pass anyone on the stairs.

We shared mints, we compared phone cases – one of us thought all that rather childish, but still we couldn't help envying that iPhone with a silver unicorn case – and we squeezed each other's hands when the flight attendant wasn't looking.

And when a man in grey trousers and creased shirt turned round to spot where the laughing came from, the bravest among us leaned forward and said, 'It's our first holiday without our parents.' The man nodded, smiled before turning back to his in-flight magazine.

That old world was small beneath us, disappearing in a misting of clouds. Most of us weren't sorry to see it go, but a few of us left something behind on the airport tarmac – that sweet tasting confidence. But none of us had any doubts about the glory waiting for us. How were we to know that not all of us would live to travel by plane again? We would all hear them of course, come to fear what they carried, the bombs waiting to fall. But all that was still to come.

All of us knew that what we had left behind could never be enough, not for us. So, we took planes, and buses, and trains, and taxis to reach our new home, the promised place. The youngest of us was only fourteen, but with a gaze steady enough, a will strong enough to hold up her eighteen-year-old cousin's passport and say to whoever asked, 'Yes, that's me.' All heading for that border. An invisible line, from one life to another, that we couldn't wait to cross.

We said to each other, Our lives are just waiting to begin.

When the first of us arrived, there was a great celebration. Men fired shots high up into the air, and some of us let our hearts soar too – this was what we were promised in the online chat rooms, the secret WhatsApp groups, the Facebook postings, the whispering to friends in the girls' toilet at school. One of us would, at the moment of the first bang, realise that this was all a mistake, that we should have stayed close to our mother, that our father really wasn't so bad, that the boss at the shoe shop wasn't the worst boss in the world. One of us, after the second volley, couldn't keep our hands from shaking, and they never stopped, not after the first marriage, nor the second, not with the birth of the first son, not even at death as the earth cracked and swallowed us up with our sons and second husband encased in brick, mortar, dust, and each other's arms.

When more of us arrived – this was much later – the gunfire wasn't wasted on the clouds, and each bullet was meant to find its target. But all were welcomed: 'Sister, this way,' the Brothers said. 'Sister, you are honoured in this our land.' Brothers said, 'Sister, we prayed you would arrive and now you are here. We are blessed.'

We wanted these men as our Brothers and our husbands. Some of us already hoped the dark-skinned man with the red bandana tied around his head would be looking for a wife. But one of our Sisters, who had already been there a month, said he was destined for eternity: tomorrow he would go out and conquer the city walls off on the horizon. And that made us long for him more. Even after we were married, when our husband climbed on top, it was that dark-skinned man and the flash of red bandana we imagined above us.

We had work to do. We the blessed, we alone were brave enough to find this land. Some of us did it without the help of our brothers or fathers. Some of us came with husbands, following them, led by them without even knowing this was where we were heading. Most of us were young although one of us had just turned forty-two, leaving a daughter behind (didn't she prefer her father anyway) but bringing with us a son who ran everywhere carrying a plastic gun, shouting out, 'Bang bang. You're dead'.

Some of us came with a sister, a cousin, a friend, someone we could link arms with, someone to hold us up when we fell to our knees and cried that first night, away from that old home, from the tumble of traffic outside the window, from the snoring of younger siblings, from the tuneless hum of our mother picking up socks, stacking away dishes, washing down countertops. We were pleased to have someone to wipe away the tears when we sobbed that we would never be able to sleep again without those familiar sounds.

But there we all were. We the chosen ones.

We spent those first days and first weeks in a fizz of excitement.

We walked the narrow lengths of street that inched forward each day: a new road here; a new house gained at that turn. And if the streets weren't as clean as we hoped, if the dust made our eyes itch, and the lack of street lights made us wake in the night, gasping for breath, thinking the world had collapsed on our head, then it was only because this home was new, must be sweated over, bled over, cried over, before it could reach full bloom. Even those of us who'd never left the grey packed streets of Berlin, of London, of Paris, we still knew that life waited to burst forth from those towns and villages that we, us and our Brothers, gathered around us. The burned-out shops, the torn-apart school, those things had to be, for new life to come forth. And if the streets were empty but for stumps and rubble and tanks, well, we saw the fig trees, the nesting starlings, the potted geraniums on windowsills that would one day return.

We had purpose. We were important. No one to laugh and say, 'You can't do that'. No one to point and say, 'Do that'. No one to shout over the wall, down the phone, through the door, 'You're worthless.' 'You're a slut.' 'Get back where you belong.'

We belonged here.

It was our choice. Some of us had too much choice: these clothes or those clothes; exams or apprenticeship. Some of us never had any choices, rubbish school, rubbish handouts, no better off than the parents who dragged us away from homelands we'd never visited. One of us even regretted the choice to get on that plane, but we would also come to regret trying to leave this place when the Brothers caught us later on.

There was a hospital, a distribution centre, an armoury, a recruitment centre. It was very organised. Sometimes the lights didn't work. Sometimes there was nothing to distribute. Usually there wasn't enough anaesthetic. Some of us thought not everything was as we had hoped it would be. But most of us were happy to be there.

We each had a job to do, things couldn't always go smoothly, but we were content. It's true that we cried the first time we saw the blood. But we would learn to be strong. Some of us had more than enough strength and laughing we picked up a stick and beat anyone not covered correctly, anyone who whispered bad things about us behind their hands.

Some of us sent out encrypted messages: *Come, all welcome. Meet us in Paradise. We need you.* Electronic pulses, codes as intricate and beautiful as butterflies that turned to dust if anyone tried to catch them. *For your eyes only.*

We had so much to do. We believed it all, believed so hard. Our Brothers said, 'You are warriors.' Our Brothers said, 'You are great.' But we knew our Brothers waited for us to fulfil our true purpose.

We had to populate this new world of ours. Most of us were happy to do it, to have someone to hold, someone we could belong with, someone familiar in this new longed for (so longed for) but strange world.

Some of us wrote out a list: nineteen to twenty-five; English or French speaker; no widowers. Some of us counted the things we wanted on our fingers, tapping out our longing: kind; good fighter; under thirty. One of us said there was a boy we already knew; his name was _____. We were taken to the Brothers who told us not to speak that name again, that the boy we knew was a spy for the enemy, no one wanted to think we were spies too.

We never spoke that boy's name again, not until we lay on a stretcher in the hospital with shrapnel working its way to our heart, and his name slipped out in a last prayer.

We all had husbands delivered to us. If he was nearer to forty than the twenty-five we requested, these were only small things. And if on our first night together he left fingerprint bruises on us (inside and out) then things would be better when we knew each other. For we could never now be separated, not even in death. Though death did come.

Many of us married more than once; a few of us married more than twice. They had brief, bright and burning lives our husbands. Some of us were even happy to see them gone (not that we spoke this above a whisper). We remembered the night they branded us with the back of a machete. The red scar still sat on the underside of our right breast, and when we nursed our daughter, we were sure she winced at our pain when she grabbed for our scarred flesh.

For most of us, the babies came. Some of us felt a slickness between our thighs and the first not quite child slipped between the cracks of the tiled floor, or down into the drainage ditch that always flooded in the rain. We learned not to cry about these small losses when so many great men's lives were at stake.

Some of us had beautiful sons and daughters that we worshipped (secretly) and husbands who held them up in the air and promised them a wonderful life where everyone believed as we did, who lived as we did, who would never cross the road to avoid us, spit beer in our faces, or tell us they knew best. But some of us, when we closed our eyes, could still picture our old neighbours – they weren't the same as *us* – but they used to give packets of crisps to all the kids in the street, they bounced oranges out of their hands into ours, they mended our bikes, re-fitted the handles of our skipping ropes. Would such neighbours be allowed to live in the new world we were building?

Some of us tried to stay off the streets. We were never sure what might fall from the sky. Didn't we see one time a man plummeting head first? No, that was just a bundle of rags. One of us knew the man who fell; we told our husband how we caught him admiring the new boyish recruits. Such evils have no place, the Brothers said. We nodded, we said, No evils. Some of us dreaded who would be next to fall. And some of us, the more the cleansings went on, the dirtier we felt. Standing under the rigged-up hose in the crumbling house where we lived, we rubbed our skin until it burned red, we bit our nails down to the bed (trying to get out all the filth trapped there).

Others knew this to be the true way, for the punishment to be just, and we slept soundly beside our husbands, only grumbling and waking when the bombs fell, or the gunfire came too close.

We didn't sleep much. We slept all day and couldn't get up, not even when our husbands kicked the bed and called us any number of names. We worried that the bombing launched dust and poison that got into our baby's lungs. Hear him wheeze. The doctor nodded, the helpers nodded, but no one had the medicine to fix him.

We worried that the bombs had shaken our brains loose because into our dreams slipped memories of that place we left, that old home. We saw the kebab shop where we got skinny fries. We saw the hardware store that sold phone cases all the colours of the rainbow, cats and smiley faces.

On the street the next day, we saw a shattered iPhone case. We picked it up, rubbed it with our fingers. It was a silver unicorn, and we remembered the girl we sat with on the plane, and we wondered if she needed the phone case back and we felt bad for hoping, back then, that the phone would break, that the case would shatter – it was a time, back then, when we thought such things were important. Now we just lived to conquer.

Some of us picked up guns, knives, sticks and stones.

Some of us washed down concrete courtyards with buckets of hot water: swilling blood, grey matter, splinters of bone out into the dusty streets.

Some of us pretended not to notice that in the bins were heads – we bleached, we scrubbed, buffed the metal back to a bin.

We had important work to do, we told ourselves that, and some of us came close to believing it was still true.

The food we were promised didn't come. The medicine we were promised didn't come. One of us said that this world was not what it should be, that our Brothers had corrupted what was such a good cause. One of us planned to leave that night, and we made it to the next town, but the Brothers found us; we were easy to spot running through the rubble holding that belly with a ripe baby inside.

'You're not worthy,' the Brothers said. The Brothers said, 'We must set an example.' Said, 'Careful of the baby – not her body.' The Brothers burned our fingers, broke our toes. 'You're a traitor,' the Brothers said. The baby was born the next day.

We knew then that we were not special, we were not great.

We were lost.

Some of us would never believe that, not even when our husbands brought home a skinny eleven-year-old girl. Devil, he called her. We said nothing when he beat her. We said nothing when he took her to his bed each night. And when he got ready to take her back to market for an exchange, only then did we speak to her. We dug the contraceptive pill packet out of the sock, hidden in the mattress, that the doctor at the hospital had smuggled to us after we lost the second baby and nearly lost all of our blood. Do you bleed? we asked her. I bleed every night, she said. Take these, we said, keep them hidden but take them. She nodded. She was exchanged, and we never saw her again, not even in our sweat-soaked nightmares did *her* face appear.

It will never end, some of us said.

Some of us ran until the enemy surrounded us.

Some of us gave up without a fight, holding our babies close, shielding our husbands.

Some of us slipped over borders, waiting in far off towns for a moment to return to where we started, hoping that the dream was not really dead, that from the embers...

One of us aimed a gun and shot our three sleeping children and then ourselves.

Most of us headed or were herded to camps. We held close a child that wasn't ours; her mother once told us a story about a school visit to a chicken factory, how it all seemed so sanitary, so cellophane clear, but behind the metal doors at the back of the factory floor, there lurked a bloody guts smell, a cracking and ripping of necks that even the massive machinery couldn't hide. We kept that little girl with us: we washed her, loved her even, but hated her too for living when our own children had starved. She lay beside us at night, screeching like a creature being gutted, and if we let go of her, she would run round and round the tent then stop, slamming her body to the dirt floor like a headless chicken searching for escape.

Outside the tents, high in the darkening sky, we saw aeroplanes. Some of us remembered that planes could carry passengers not just drop bombs. We remembered that day we travelled to a new life. But most of us kept our eyes down on the ground.

Now we wait.

We do not know what we are waiting for.

There they are again in the newspaper, let them stay printed in ink. Don't let them back. They've committed crimes, treason, more than that – full of hatred for anything they don't believe in. Hate is all they have.

Keep out.

Those faces and black gowns will be tomorrows rubbish on the street. Good riddance. Better out there than where decent people have to see them. The child, the child of the child that is, well that's a shame, but their mothers should have thought of that.

Keep your friends close, your enemies closer – perhaps there's something to be said for it. Only the joy of punishment, of 'Serve's you right', is so much stronger. What's a passport to them anyway? They're not stateless, they chose a state, and now it will be crushed back into dust and sand and rubble.

They made their bed.

They showed no pity, and now they'll get none. Don't let their hate get blown on the wind to settle in cracks and crevices of some other unstable place – until they come to our door.

Stay away.

They're worse than criminals. Animals. A much bigger crime, a much bigger punishment. They have to be accountable for the things they did, even the things they did as children.

On Broadway

On Broadway he ploughs his cart like Columbus across the seas. Legs wrapped in black plastic, hair plaited with dirt. The Stars and Stripes – left over from someone else's party – billow around his shoulders. He keeps his eyes lowered; rescues a rolling Coke from the sidewalk. The tourists, in bright T-shirts, trot out of his way, and the office suits, who pass him every day, pass again. But they all bite their lips and hold their breath against the unwashed nightmare of him: redundancy, home repossession. He shakes the last dregs and a cigarette butt from the can, before bedding it down into his collection. The hermetically sealed traffic swerves around him. The hollering horns and the hiss of a thousand swerving yellow taxis can't reach him.

His fingertips brush the roped-up bags of treasure. He smiles at the tinkle and crunch of aluminium as the cart bumps over hot tarmac. From the red and white of a Friday Bud to the bright green of a Sunday morning Mountain Dew: all the company he needs. No iPhone app to navigate for him; Google Maps can't plot the route his folks took all those years before when they heard the call of the American Dream. They tried to answer with accents thick as molasses and up-jumbled words. Nobody heard them.

He shouts, a single syllable warning, as a truck tramples too close. He shields the cart with his body. The flag catches in the updraft and tightens around his neck.

One day, when he is ready, he will swap those cans for crisp bucks, and he'll be on his way. Until then he keeps the cart moving; one more sail fluttering against the wind.

They Were the Only Ones Dancing

I wasn't there myself, but my neighbour told me all about it. Things like that stick in your mind, he said. And he'd seen many things in Peckham during his many years. They weren't from around here, he said. He never used to think of me as local but what with all the table tennis bars, rooftop cocktails, and artisan flour dusting the shop fronts, he must have decided ten years in the flat above him meant I'd served my apprenticeship.

It was gone eight o'clock, another Friday night in The Hope (between the phone shop and the halal butchers), when it happened. A hotter than usual May evening. Paving slabs creaked in the heat, pigeons bathed in dust, and buses glinted with reflections of the setting sun streaked across their windows. Darkness was coming to Rye Lane, but it wouldn't bring any relief from the concrete and brick-soaked heat.

My neighbour was sitting on his usual stool, second from the right; far enough away from the fruit machine that the rattle of silver wouldn't remind him of the sound his settling dentures made when dropped into the tumbler at night. The daylight never quite pierced the greasy windows and thick red upholstery of The Hope; he squinted into the bottom of his glass. A draught scratched the untrimmed hair at the back of his neck.

He downed the rum; swivelling around on the stool to face the door. Three blokes, in running shoes with soles so white they must have been scrubbed with bleach, strutted in. They wore a uniform of white T-shirts and dark jeans. It wasn't anyone he knew. My neighbour tapped his foot on the rung; he'd wasted his last drop in the hope of a free top-up.

He had been chasing Guinness with Navy Rum at The Hope for going on twenty years. The other drinkers at the bar had been there for nearly as long. He used to go every Tuesday, Friday, and Saturday lunchtime, with his wife. After she passed, he always stayed until late.

Surfacing onto Rye Lane in the early hours took some swift footwork, even for those who hadn't had two or three shots to keep off the chill. All along Rye Lane, butchers took right of way. Meat stock arrived early in the morning, wheeled in supermarket trolleys, hoisted out of white vans. Beef carcasses and goat legs piled on newspaper and wooden pallets. Sidestepping deliveries was the closest anyone got to dancing on those streets. So much life already lived before the papers arrived, before the station opened, when birds nestling on the edges of Rye Common welcomed a false dawn, confused by the orange pulse of the streetlamps. My neighbour liked a lock-in.

And that's when I usually heard him: when yesterday edged its way towards tomorrow. He played records until the grey dawn trickled through his nets; sepia-tinted, unwashed since his wife died. The crackle of the needle sounded like cicadas; the tropics come alive in Peckham. Mento, Ska, Blues, weaving threads of walking bass, and high rhythms; rising up into my dreams.

The pub jukebox was all Foster and Allen, Elvis Presley, my neighbour said. Nothing was playing that night in May, just the ding ding of the fruit machine. But the jukebox was in the middle of the pub, between the brown varnished tables and the brass-studded bar. Whenever new blokes made a play for the place, setting out to own it, they started by controlling the music. That was what those three youths in bright whites and dark jeans did. They went and stood by the jukebox.

My neighbour said he'd seen it happen before. Gangs came and went, and weren't they all after the same thing – a nice, quiet place to sup? White curls, a dent in the stool padding that perfectly matched his rear, meant his orders always got served and his routine never got disrupted. He thought he'd seen it all from that stool, but before the night was through, he would be proved wrong.

Those youths leaned against the jukebox, not ordering, not even speaking. A glance at the bar satisfied them that the landlady, Cheryl, and the three old-timers lined up like milk bottles next to my neighbour, weren't worth a second look. The three blokes jostled against each other and the box; rearranging an elbow, straightening a knee, puffing out a chest. They eyed the tables, stretched in a line from the window to the bar.

A hot Friday night in May and the place was nearly full. A mixed crowd of those waiting to catch the number twelve bus to a club, those set for a heavy night of pint after pint, and the quiet drinkers out to escape the silence of their own four walls. It wasn't just men. Women in sleeveless tops, with strong arms and wide backs, took their share of seats; toes and ankles out for spring, budding like bright primroses on Peckham Rye Common.

One of the young blokes came back to the jukebox with three pints wedged between his hands. They drank. The men at the tables were starting to turn, ears burning, necks itching – knowing they were watched. My neighbour was about to get back to his *Racing Times*, order another rum, when the door opened. A couple came in.

Something about the couple made him lean back against the bar, loosen the button behind his tie like he'd just eaten rice and peas, dumplings, and curry (heavy and sweet – just how his wife used to make it). The couple were arm in arm. Her in a flowering-rose tea dress, him in a blue checked waistcoat and yellow shirt.

The way from the door, past the tables, into the pub was narrow. The couple stepped closer together rather than pull apart. Her silver patent shoes pooled like mercury waiting for the temperature to rise. The couple headed for the jukebox. The man's thin waxed moustache coming to light under the beams above the bar. My neighbour couldn't hear what the couple said, but the three blokes at the jukebox sniggered, gulped down the last of their drinks. The blokes shifted a little to the left, and the couple took their time scrolling through song titles.

A big-band tune thumped to life. The couple placed their hands on shoulders and hips, merging together. Feet finding a rhythm, clicking and tapping on the parquet. The brass trim around the carpet made them step off each time they came to an edge, like waltzers spinning round and round the square of exposed floor.

They were the only ones dancing.

Their Peckham wasn't his, passing like ghosts – was it always that way? The dancers held each other close, the music played. They circled in and out of the flashing beams of the jukebox; cartwheels of red and green like out-of-control traffic lights – stop/go.

One of the blokes, with a cockerel emblem stitched to his T-shirt, thumped the jukebox with his fist. But the music didn't stop. Some of the men at the tables began to point and laugh. They rubbed sweat and gelled hair back from their foreheads.

All that rage circling like water stains on the tabletops, but the dancing couple didn't notice. They didn't know they were watched; they didn't know the pub bristled. Their temples touched. My neighbour thought, even above the electric hiss of the jukebox, he heard that meeting of skin and skin, soft and damp as a kiss.

The dancing couple weren't listening to the orchestra of teeth sucking, knuckle cracking, lost as they were in the rhythm of the dance. One of the young blokes, with razor cuts in his hair and pumps that looked two sizes too big, made a move towards the tables. He stepped onto the dance floor. A chair got knocked backwards. A man at the tables jumped up. They stared at each other like dogs in the street. Each thinking himself cock of the walk.

Well, it's funny, that sort of posturing, until it's not. My neighbour didn't know who threw the first pint-glass. It smashed on the hardwood floor, skittering shards. The dancing couple stepped apart, caught either side of the men. They looked around them for the first time. They didn't know there were places you shouldn't go into; they didn't know you should never walk in the front without knowing how to get out the back.

My neighbour stood up, not to break apart the fight, but to tell that couple, Keep dancing. Please, keep dancing. But no words came out. He grasped the velvet-covered stool. It couldn't hold him. Hot striking pain, scorching him from hair roots to toes; felling him like a lightning-struck London plane tree.

Before my neighbour slumped to the floor, he saw the dark chimneys of Tilbury Docks, standing tall like stripped palm trees, he saw the steam-fair swings rise high above the Rye, he saw grass flood the Grand Surrey Canal submerging it into Burgess Park. So many things he saw, but the last was that dancer's patent leather shoes, sparkling silver; in those he saw himself reflected, not as an old man, but as he was once.

He told me all about it when I visited him at King's College Hospital. I went the first time out of pity. I took in his post, watered his spider plants, brought him grapes he didn't eat, and Lucozade that he spilled on his flannel pyjamas. The green blanket was tucked tight around him, pinning him. His hands were free. The left floated above the sheet, moving like a branch in the wind, fingers tapping air as he described everything to me. How her silver shoes glistened, not crinkled like foil but bright and clear as a mirror. How the thin hairs of the man's moustache, must have been brushed smooth with a toothbrush – a redness to the tips like the henna his wife had used on her hair.

I visited him on the ward every evening that week. When he spoke about the dancing couple, about the pub, about the thrown glass, he held my hand in his right hand. We'd done no more than smile in the common hallway before that. I asked him about how the dancing couple moved, about how they held each other close. I wanted what they had, and like a patient teacher, he told me all he knew.

On my last visit, he pulled me close, whispered in my ear, Why were they the only ones dancing?

The second stroke took him in the early hours of the following Saturday. No fighting it, no re-generation for all.

There was a wake at The Hope, but no one mentioned the couple who had danced so close, how her silver shoes shone, and his waxed moustache was polished as the countertop. Perhaps they were the only ones to have ever danced on that square of parquet between the sticky topped tables and the fruit machine.

By the time the barista and the potter moved into the downstairs flat, I had changed my walk home from the accounting office. It took an extra seven minutes to go past the pub doors, but I did it each day. Every time I paused to stare through the windows at the velvet bar stools, the hardwood floor, the dark red centre of the place.

I never saw any dancing.

The Hope is gone now, refitted as a Paddy Power betting shop. And my neighbour, he's buried in Nunhead Cemetery, beside his wife. I rescued his record collection from the skip, uploaded those crackling sounds to my iPod. When I lie in bed, listening to Prince Buster's 'One Step Beyond' or The Skatalites 'Freedom March', through the window I can see the green graveside trees waving. We'll be neighbours again one day.

Back Issues

He keeps the *Exchange and Mart* open on his knees. The wind tries to steal it, but he's not letting go. He has more in his bag; can't separate the months – that would be bad luck. The copy he has is for January 1950. The Austin Princess, his first family car. A gift from his parents on the birth of his son. All his firstborn, his little girl, got was a silver spoon. His parents were old fashioned sorts.

He picks another copy from his bag, reads the listings for Ford Transit vans. He used to have a dream of leaving his job, packing up the children, the dogs, and along with his wife they would see the world together. He knows all the adverts by heart, but one is circled, the one he meant to get: 1963, taxed and insured, reasonable offers accepted. But his wife was back studying the law; she didn't have time for his dreams. He never made an offer on any of those vans.

A young boy in shorts runs past the bench, shouting and waving his arms as if he means to take flight. Is that his boy? Where's his girl? Where is his wife? So many children in Dulwich Park, he can't be blamed for not picking out his own flesh and blood. They'll come back when they're hungry.

There's a man on the other end of the bench, a paper cup of tea between them. He's thirsty, thinks the drink must be his and helps himself. His wife probably left it for him. It's so hard to keep track of them all these days.

His wife will be somewhere doing the crossword, or those Japanese square things with numbers missing.

He shakes his head, squints against the low sunlight.

He has lots of gaps.

But not in his collection of *Exchange and Mart*, which stops when they switched to that net thing; like Technicolor ruined the precision of black and white. It's the paper he likes; he rubs a page between his fingers, soft as winceyette pyjamas.

The past isn't gone; it's all in these back issues.

He closes his eyes. Yesterday is so much easier to see than tomorrow. He reaches into his satchel, runs a finger down a spine in the bag; a static pulse.

Everyone needs backbone.

He pulls out September 1947. Page two, Triumph 3T motorcycle. He got it for a song. Such a good bike, clung to every corner, well, all except one. The break in his leg still aches when it rains.

He looks up. It's not raining now, or the red and black ink would soak into his skin. The transferred words would sit in his palm, makes and models catalogued inside him – he should have liked a tattoo, but his mother and father never would have approved of that, although his wife might have liked it.

Barbara wasn't the wife his mother wanted for him. His mother kept clippings of debutantes and women who loved horses, leaving them under his breakfast plate. Barbara's family were trade – which made them worse than the Germans in his mother's eyes.

But Barbara, Barbara, she was always the one. They went on honeymoon to a caravan her dad had built, anchored on a van base; shipwrecked on Southend sandbars. Three days of heaven. It wasn't the first time they'd seen all of each other – Barbara wasn't the old-fashioned sort. But it was the first time he ever saw her feet. He can still feel them in his hands.

Air-dried and toasty as teacakes. The colours blend, veins run close to the surface of her sun-soaked skin. Two feet that have been places, travelled roads and paddled in oceans, steeped in sunny days of ice cream and summer rain. Toenails that are white and pink against the flesh, like seaside candyfloss.

Each time her feet touch his, the slide of skin on skin rubs life into him.

He could lie head to tail with her all day and stare at those feet. He breathes in the scent of warm skin, comforting as the smell of baking bread. And when he reaches out and touches her soles, the skin down there feels like layers of paper beneath his fingertips, and he reads her.

When she pulls on socks and shoes, his body aches to see her bareness again, draw her close to him. The muscles that move, the motion that washes through her feet shouldn't be hidden. There should be a word to describe the movement; the infinitive 'to walk' disregards the role. Footing or feeting – something like fleeting.

He calls out, 'Barbara?'

No answer. He reaches into his bag. Another time. March 1986. Scanning rising pricing for *cherished plates*. But this copy is all wrong. The edges are torn, little shreds flutter between his fingers. He shakes his head, but the image of a grey-flecked woman enters beside him. She stands in the middle of the room, kicks at the toppling piles of *Exchange and Mart*. Stands between him and his back issues. Calls herself wife. It's wrong, all wrong.

He stands up. 'Barbara, where are you?'

The man on the bench answers. 'She's not here.'

'Then fetch her, man. I must see my wife.'

'She's gone.'

'Who are you to say such a thing?'

'Come on, Dad. Let's put your shoes and socks back on. I'll take you home.'

All wrong, all so wrong.

He shuts his eyes, takes himself back to the end of all this and the beginning of all that:

Elbows on glass counter, a chill about his knees, not old enough for long trousers. He counts out ha'pennies.

Spring rain tapping at WH Smith's window.

The shopkeeper slips his copy of *Exchange and Mart* into a bag – lifted, not torn from the hook – hands it over.

He cradles it tight to his chest, crinkling thud of his heart against brown paper.

Issue number one. Mint condition. One careful owner.

A Glimmer of Melting Ice

Ivy, who was now two years a widow, lay alone in bed. She gripped the front of her nightshirt; her skin thin and creased as the cotton. Maybe this would be the day. She'd waited long enough.

In the distance, firecrackers boomed and snapped; the children from the next farm starting the June celebrations early. Part of Ivy wished she was that age again, to not remember two world wars, to not know what people could do to each other. Another shower of cracks and bangs. Something hit the window. A greasy halo was imprinted on the glass. The children's noise had scared a bird out of the sky.

Ivy wanted to know if it had flown free. She inched her legs over the side of the bed, but her feet didn't touch the rug. Recently she had found herself shrinking like ice left in the sun, smaller than she was as a young thing. Maybe that was the way it should be – one day she would slip away, nothing but a glimmer of melting ice. She slid to standing, keeping hold of the crocheted quilt.

A snuffling sound came from the other side of the bed. For too long now it had been only her in those embroidered sheets. Ivy rested against the iron bedstead.

A baby lay in a crib. The baby wasn't hers; Ivy knew that. It must be a Sunday because she had the feeling the house was full; the old, weathered boards creaking at holding so much life. But no, it was Fête Nationale, the firecrackers told her that. Her sons and daughters, their husbands and wives, children, were all downstairs – busy tending new families.

She stroked the baby's cheek; its eyelashes fluttering in sleep – picturing so many things, things not seen, not lived, but waiting. The pink ribbon threaded on the gown, a little girl of course. Ivy's first granddaughter after five grandsons. Eirwen never got to meet this little one.

Ivy wrapped her arms around what was left of herself. Just as she did every day on waking, all through 1953 and now into 1954, she wished Eirwen was beside her. She shuffled over to the window. He'd been gone for two years, the longest lifetime lived, and everything now, without him, was cloudy and dimmed like the old panes in the window.

Ivy put her shoulder under the window sash, heaved it up a little. Cornfields, stretching wide as a sea, bristling with sunshine; that was one of the things she always loved about the farm – flat for miles, seeing anyone coming before they even knew which way they were heading. She breathed in the dusty musk of trampled corn husks, but beneath that ran a current of air as clean and cool as a china plate.

The lake slept beyond the horizon. Blue and bright at this time of year but just waiting for the first white freeze. The Huron's called it Lake of Shining Waters. Eirwen always said it should be called Lake of Shining Ice. She should like to see it again.

Ivy leaned out. But the lake was past the fields encircling the house, and the red barn blocked the view. She thought, for a moment, that someone stood beside the barn doors beckoning to her, but no it was just the shimmering heat. She longed for the cold creep of winter, the clarity of snow and ice; things could be seen clearly then.

Ivy held onto the window frame. She rubbed her aching arm. The barn's shingle roof peeled and blistered; it needed sealing. One of the boys would do it; there was really no need for her to tell them. The young liked to think everything was their own idea. But she did come to the window for a reason. The bird – had it flown free? It wasn't on the sill. Ivy peered over the ledge. She could be out of that window and away, and falling might feel like flying. A shock of colour caught her eye.

Down on the porch roof it lay, wings spread. The iridescent blue feathers on the white wood reminded her of some earlier time – a flash of bright wings down in the coldness. And like a crack in the ice of her memory, preserved so clearly, Ivy sees again...

She sees Eirwen waiting at the end of Alaska Street in South London; smiling, eyes creased, hands on hips. 'You found me,' he says.

She stops herself from skipping over the cobbles. 'Just followed the trains out of Waterloo.' She points as one chugs over the viaduct.

Eirwen and Ivy stand facing each other between the archway workshops and factories. The hoot and thumping of the train making it impossible to speak and be heard. Is she still smiling? She's been standing still for what feels like forever – what if she is frowning? What would Eirwen think of that? He widens his grin in return. He lifts his eyebrows higher as if he has forgotten to blink. Or maybe he is surprised to see her, surprised she came. It must be the longest train in the world passing by.

A little mole sits on his cheek just below his left eye, like a smudged teardrop – she hasn't noticed that before. He must be studying her too. She thinks her nose too short, her eyelashes too short, her height too short, and her chin too wide. But that doesn't seem to matter when he looks at her. She smiles on.

They are laughing now, she doesn't know who started it, and just as quickly the train is gone. The laughter gone, leaving behind silence thick as coal dust. Ivy isn't sure she can ever speak again. Something lodges in her mouth, constricts her ribs; she is only eighteen, but in this frozen moment she feels herself so old. Eirwen rubs his throat; he must feel it too. He gives a cough, turning aside to do it, clearing the quiet out of himself.

He speaks first, 'Don't tell me your answer yet.' She tries to speak, but he shakes his head. 'I want to show you something. If you tell me no, I ain't going to want to do it, and if you tell me yes, you'll think I showed you this to make you not regret your choice.' He shakes his head again at the jumble of words. 'Just come with me.'

Ivy follows him towards the end of the street. The back of his head, his long neck, are worth looking at, but she doesn't know what else there could be to see in this dirty, deserted place.

Eirwen stops by an archway with wooden doors big as castle gates. A train rumbles into Waterloo station. It smokes and steams, rattling the hanging chains on the archway doors. *Ice Warehouse*, frozen in blue lettering on the crumbling bricks. He presses his shoulder against a narrow opening, a door within a door, jiggling until it gives way. He holds it open for Ivy.

The door snaps shut behind them. Sun shines through the grill at the top of the gate, cutting thick lines of light across the brick floor. The black tips of Eirwen's hair turn to flames in the last of the afternoon brightness. Ivy pivots in the light, letting it bathe her. She thinks she might like to stand here forever.

Eirwen steps away, touching her arm. 'This way,' he says, heading into the shade of the tunnel.

Ivy hesitates. The drip drip of water running down the walls, a prickling of hair at the back of her neck as if someone breathes behind her, whispering, *This way change lies.*

Eirwen calls to her, the tunnel deepens his voice. Ivy chases after his echo. Either side of the red brick walls stand lines of what look like big quarry blocks, enough to build a small town. Eirwen's silhouette disappears in the foggy gloom.

Dark stack after stack, covered in sacking, line the curved walls, reaching up to the arch of the ceiling. The way narrows, but something glows at the end: silvery blue like spilt mercury. Eirwen's outline covers the path, the shadows making him appear bigger than he is. Ivy slips in beside him. She rubs warmth back into her cold, aching arms. Their breath hangs in a dense mist about their heads, but it tastes sweet and crisp like the air in Victoria Park after a downpour.

Eirwen rests his elbow on a block. He reaches out, tugs on the sacking. It swishes to the floor.

Ivy shields her eyes from the glow. 'Ice,' she says.

The brightest light she's ever seen. Their reflections merge into one smudged form, only separating when Eirwen drags away more brown sacking from a block beside her.

'Comes all the way from Canada,' he says, proud as if he dragged it across land himself. 'Nothing clearer.'

He presses his nose to the ice, staring deep into it. Ivy does the same. Anyone gazing so deep might hope to see a fairytale parade of lives, of families, of cities and streets. Ivy sees herself, sees the back of Eirwen's head. Beyond, she sees fields of yellow, a deep blue lake, children, snowshoes, boats, a barn. She sees so many things preserved and waiting in the ice.

She peels herself away; her nose throbs with the cold. She stands back again. The ice shines brighter still; buried inside is all the light of the world.

'Come, look from up here,' Eirwen says.

He reaches for a ladder, grimy with grease, and it doesn't seem right to let it touch the sharp angles and sides. But Eirwen already has the top rung hooked over the ledge above. Giant block upon giant block, sleeping on cushions of straw and wooden boards to ferry the melt away. He takes the rungs two at a time.

Ivy wants to go with him, won't let herself be left behind. The ladder shakes, but she keeps climbing. The worn soles of Eirwen's boots in front of her. The cracks must let in the damp and the chill, and his trousers catch on the top of his boots. The skin around his ankles is goosebumped. He needs a thick pair of woollen socks.

He pants lightly from the cold and the steepness of the climb. Ivy's toes and fingers stiffen, turning numb. Her foot slips, she holds on. She knows she can follow him all the way to the top.

Eirwen hangs out from the ladder, looking down. 'I won't let you fall.'

Ivy nods, keeps her attention on the worn wood. And before she reaches him, she has a feeling, that something inside the ice, something of her reflection, is looking back, that she's inside the ice.

Eirwen takes hold of her hand, helps her step out onto the flat table of ice. They are at the very top. Ivy smiles, reaches up, runs her fingertips along the brick roof. 'We're standing on the very edge, aren't we?'

He smiles, kneels on the ice. 'I saw it in your smile,' he says, tucking his hands under his armpits, warming them. 'We're getting that boat.'

The air is too cold to let her blushes show. Ivy presses her fingertips to her lips, warming them with her breath. She kneels next to him. Sunlight drips through the grill above their heads, and above that lies the train tracks that will take them to the docks, take them to the boat which will soon set sail for Canada. A whole new beginning, their new life – Ivy saw it all in the ice.

A train rumbles over; the block vibrates under them. Ivy puts out a hand to steady herself – something stares back, lodged under the surface. She rubs at it with the edge of her skirt, buried too deep to reach. The ice polishes up like glass, revealing what was hidden: a bird with wings spread as if it soars. The feathers glow deep blue and black, white-tipped, spread apart like fingers. The delicate head turned on its side, eye open. And things like that mean something, don't they, shouldn't they? Eirwen scratches at it with his nail. He says, 'I've never seen a bird like it. Must have been struck down through the grating.'

'Or come all the way from Canada,' she says.

The ladder creaks, the ice sighs like the distant whoosh of flocking birds. Ivy presses her ear closer. Thud thud like a heartbeat. She chips at a corner of the block, sucking the sliver off her finger. It tastes of fresh air, a whistling sharpness over her teeth. Ivy scratches at the block again, holding up a crystal for Eirwen.

He sucks it straight off her outstretched hand. The heat of his mouth shocks her. He licks her palms, one after another. Ivy shivers. He laughs as he sticks both her hands to the ice. Water collects in drops on the side of the block. No sound now but the drip drip of water. He rests his head on her shoulder. Her hands float free. She stares at his ridged knuckles, wondering what they will look like next to her skin. The heat coming out of his palms flowers through her. One breath and Ivy will warm that ice back into rain.

'We'll always be together,' he says.

The top of his head presses against her neck. She melts a little lower, nudging his hair with her chin, the curls soft and springy. He raises his face, slowly blinking. The amber and hazel flecks in his eyes pool into black as he comes closer.

Ivy feels that bird trapped inside her, battering against her stomach. *Don't let it out, don't let it fly away,* she wants to shout. But there isn't enough air left in her body. Oh God – she wants to use that name when nothing short of a prayer feels right, only she can't remember one. The ridge of Eirwen's nose is hot on her cheek. Eyelashes tickling like feathers. Can he breathe? Can she breathe? Yes. Steam comes out of them.

The dark blue of the ice glows around them.

Right on the very cracking edge now, seeing nothing but blue. She lets herself be taken – frozen in flight like that bird...

It wasn't dead; stunned and shivering, thumping its beak against the roof. The bird spread the blue lightning strike of its wings as it hopped up. A blue jay – that's what they saw all those years ago at the ice warehouse when they were little more than children.

Ivy rested her forehead on the window; a breeze circled off the fields, rattling the growing ears of corn. She wanted to feel cold again. A glass of lemonade sat on the dresser, left by one of her daughters no doubt. They always remembered she liked it loaded with ice. Ivy picked up the glass. It clicked and crackled, slowly shrinking as she watched. But ice from refrigerators could never be the same as lake ice: too riddled with bubbles and fissures, cracked and cloudy like an antique mirror. There was nothing new to see.

Ivy stumbled against the bed. Firecrackers exploded outside the barn, echoing around the house. Ivy's heart tripped over itself, soaring out of her chest. The glass broke itself on the floor. The ice skidded across the bedroom.

Ivy clutched her chest. Pumping blood and feathers; loud as the sound of running feet on the stairs. She wanted one last look, lifting her head. But her thoughts slipped out of the room.

A time traveller through her own life now. And she chose to return, back to a moment on ice...

Ivy and Eirwen stand so close that not even the Atlantic air comes between them. Most of the boat sleeps, rocked by the gentle lap of waves after days of stormy seas. They have been waiting on deck since the ringing of the bell. The moon washes them in its milky glow. The deck glistens bright as polished glass. Their breath steams.

Slowly it emerges from the darkness, rearing up from the depths, a rising cliff. Iceberg. The word freezes on their tongues. They feel as if they have slipped into the ice at the warehouse, facing that first block. A moment never to be forgotten.

The ice creaks, the wind whispers about it, shedding flakes like plumes of feathers that melt in their outstretched hands. They laugh; the chilled skin on their faces feels stretched enough to split. And what would spill out of them would be hot happiness – vivid as the strip of light opening up the horizon, bursting with a fresh dawn.

They believe it is the happiest of all times, the most there ever is to feel. If it weren't for the frozen air, the crackling brightness of it all, there would be tears of joy at such bliss. They don't yet know how sadness too will come to pass. How life, like the ice, holds so many things for them.

'Sooner or later must an end always come?' Eirwen asks.

Ivy closes her eyes, leans against his warm body, breathes in his scent of nutmeg, thinks this is answer enough, but the question remains...

Her son leaned in close. 'Mom, did you say ice? Does she want ice?'

'Of course she doesn't,' Ivy's youngest daughter said. 'Hurry,' she called out to the footsteps on the stairs.

Ivy's daughter-in-law ran into the room. But Ivy wasn't listening, and she wasn't afraid. In those last moments before her heart gave its final beat, Ivy hoped her children came to learn all that she had, an acceptance, but she trusted they wouldn't have to learn it yet. She didn't want this to be that moment: she was an old woman, and she'd lived, oh how she'd lived.

'Mom. Mom.' Ivy's daughter took her by the shoulders, cradling her.

Ivy's daughter-in-law scooped up the baby, held her high, taking her out to the landing as if the bedroom was sinking. 'Fetch the doctor!'

There were more important things than the pain in Ivy's arm, the pressure crushing her chest, the deafening thud of blood in her ears. Somewhere washed overboard all those voices in the room sank in the waves. But Ivy was lifted on the crest of a memory, of a love, of Eirwen, all lived long ago.

Finally, at her end, Ivy was together again with her love, the memory of him filling her.

Back to a moment on ice...

The winter of 1952 broke records in the province, the coldest for thirteen years. Ivy and Eirwen tread down to the lake, the fresh fall crunching between the holes of their snowshoes.

Over the years, Eirwen has developed an artist's sight for ice. Even on this last trip, with his left cataract, making that eye glacial like the lake, he can still spot the best places to cut. But this must be their last trip. Their sons told them it wasn't needed anymore, everyone had refrigerators, and their daughters warned them what the cold and damp could do to old lungs.

The buckskin pony and cart travel in front; too skittish to be ridden in winter when every noise and every scent hangs in the air. There is so much sky it forms a dome above them. They link arms, so close that not even the frozen wind, barrelling down from Hudson Bay, comes between them.

The pony's black-tipped ears twitch, nose snuffling, sending a spiral of steam high into the morning air like a smoke signal. It stops, nostrils flaring. Ivy and Eirwen come alongside. Ivy pats the pony's rump, guiding it towards the water's edge; another white bank to those who don't know better, for those who won't look.

Ivy stops, bends to study the snow. The pony and cart have momentum, moving on. Eirwen glances over his shoulder, gives her a nod. She nods back. He smiles and keeps going. When they first arrived in this country, French trappers still worked the mountains. Ivy knew enough of their ways to recognise a mountain lion's tracks: the four circles, the compressed 'M' shape of the snow. She's seen tracks before but never a mountain lion; too few, too secretive to be spotted. She prods the track with her snowshoe, the strings creaking. The paw print collapses in on itself. Fresh. The creature is probably only passing through. They should tell the neighbours to lock up their barns.

Ivy catches up with the cart, overtakes it. She bends down, scoops up a handful of snow, compacting it. Eirwen, who knows her well, scrambles to load up his own mittens. Ivy launches first. The snowball bursts against Eirwen's coat. This is what they do every winter since that very first one when they arrived off the boat. It makes them feel like children, makes them forget the pinch of arthritis, the ache of crumbling spines, and the dimness of fading eyes.

They pat each other down, clearing away the snow but really feeling for the familiar curves and angles of each other.

They rub noses, crystals of breath settling on their cheeks, feeling soft as feathers. There is still this last harvest to cut.

Ivy and Eirwen stand at the edge of the icy shore. The pier, the pine trees, the lake itself – all look carved in ice, a bright veneer that crackles when touched. Drifts of snow pile high against the struts of the jetty on one side. The other side is exposed as boiled bones.

They set to work, and the pony waits patiently. Eirwen saws, cuts, and chips the ice until his shirt and padded coat are soaked through. Ivy helps haul the blocks to the cart. They pat each other, and the pony, when the work brings them close, reassuring themselves that they aren't alone in the vastness. Ivy stops to wrap the scarf tight over Eirwen's chest, wants him to feel the touch of it as if it's her arms around him.

The cutting is done. The blocks nearly loaded. Eirwen stands with hands on hips, breathing in deeply as if trying to get his fill of the ice shavings dancing about them. Ivy runs her hand down his back. He shivers. She steps away from his side to collect up the tools. Steam rises from the pony, and from Eirwen. To Ivy, Eirwen smells of hot sweat, sugary coffee, the warm scent of nutmeg. Something catches her eye. She glances up.

The mountain lion smells him too. It sits atop the ridge, by the lightning struck pine, on the dividing line between meadow and forest. But Eirwen has his Winchester, and Ivy has no fear in her heart. They work on.

Only one last block to heave onto the back of the cart; only the pony's straps to be tied tight; only the rest of their lives to be lived. Ivy rubs at the side of a block, the wool of her mittens polishing the surface. She wants to see how she and Eirwen will grow old together, to see in the ice if they will ever have a granddaughter, and whether the roof of the red barn will last out the winter. The sun catches the block, refracting.

And whether it is the splintering of a snow-laden branch, echoing in the icy landscape, or whether someone else has spied the lion and it's the distorted crack of a gunshot that rips apart the hush, Ivy will never know. The lion darts into the woods. Blue jays, flashing silver and black, scatter up into the sky. Another crack.

The pony rears.

The straps snap, slither apart quicker than Eirwen can snatch at them.

The ice shakes, and all the rest comes undone.

The loaded blocks cascade. A squared and sharp-edged avalanche; both beautiful and terrifying. The pony rears again, screeching ice, or is that her screaming? Eirwen has no time to step aside. A half-ton block smashes into the left side of his skull. It crumples him into the snow.

Ivy skids towards him, stumbles into the ice. She grabs the scarf wrapped around his chest. She'll never lift him now. She embraces him, closes her eyes, curls against Eirwen's still warm body in the reddening snow; breathes in his fading scent of nutmeg.

The sun appears over the lake. Startled blue jays settle again in the pines. Icicles, broken free from the wreckage, begin to shimmer. Ivy sees the whole of life in a glimmer of melting ice. How quickly it is gone. She hears Eirwen's voice echo inside her: Must an end always come?

Ivy nods, and she finally knows the answer (to that question asked on a boat in the Atlantic so many years ago). She replies, 'Yes, this is what it is to be alive.'

Fences

We moved in on the 15th of December, but it was only on Christmas Eve that we first noticed him. Fence-man is what he came to be called, although neither of us remembered when. He stood in the next garden over, close enough that we saw the wind lift the thin strands of hair fluttering over his bald head. The ground was hard and grey, but he didn't have a coat or a hat. He stood with a spade in one hand and a sheet of chipboard in the other. We had a fine view of Fence-man from our dining table. His head bobbing up between the candles and reindeer decorations on our windowsill.

He propped the spade and chipboard against his leg, looked around his garden, not moving, just turning his head. We went back to our lunch, elbows tightly tucked in as we sat at the table for two. The Christmas tree was too big for the room, pushing up against the chairs, but we'd chosen it all the same, dragging it in backwards through the door, leaving a sharp trail of needles across the carpet. Our first Christmas in a new home, our first Christmas with only each other. We had the whole itinerary set, from the Christmas Eve lunch through to the New Year's Day World War II Blu-ray. Fence-man wasn't part of any plan.

Halfway through the warm quinoa and goats cheese salad entree, we saw Fence-man lean forward and piss against his rear fence. A streak of black where he wetted the panels, the only ones still standing in the derelict garden.

Our maisonette, we were very particular about telling people our new home possessed its own front door, was on the first floor. The view from the lounge window was out over the patchwork of back gardens. The bright green of downstairs' artificial lawn, the heritage grey painted summerhouse of next door, and beyond that the straw wilderness of Fence-man's domain. The weeds there were weathered by the harsh winter air, blown into tangled spirals, feathered by crackling frosts. The fence panels had blown down on the far side and were simply missing on the near side.

He just kept pissing against those two lone standing panels at the back.

We stood up to get a better look; forks left balanced on plates, mouthfuls of 'It's disgusting' and then spitting out giggles. We pressed our foreheads to the cold glass, knocked over the unlit candles, to peer closer. But what we really wanted was for him to lift his head high enough to see us at the window – to shame him. He kept his head dropped against his arm, his body bowed until he was almost C shaped; he seemed to be pissing from a deep well inside himself. We Instagrammed him with #neighboursfromhell.

It all seemed so funny back then.

Well, that first time we did laugh until we had to sit down again. The warmed salad was no longer warm; it was just a salad. Not hearty enough to keep off the December chill. Lamb's tail lettuce was turned over, lentils skated up the edges of the china, goat's cheese crusted, until the plates were pushed away. One thing crossed off our list of holiday activities, our carefully constructed framework of timeslots – for meals, for chores, for Christmassy spirit, for not thinking of other things. He might have ruined one meal, but what was that really? Fence-man was the perfect thing to make sure we forgot about the last place we lived, about the upstairs neighbour there, about what could happen when we got bored.

We topped up on port, clinked classes, congratulating ourselves on spearheading regeneration in this south-east corner of the city; for planting our flag after years of crippling rents, packed lunches and flasks of coffee. Fence-man was a bit of a laugh, a joke, something to talk about after we'd consumed another boxset on Netflix and waited for the migraine rush of brightness and blare to subside.

We laughed all through Christmas. Always rushing to a window when we heard Fence-man working his way out to his garden.

It would start with him shouting at his wife, sometimes he'd have to chase one of his boys away from the shed, then the pacing, the banging, the measuring would go on until his wife yelled at him (sometimes hours later, sometimes only when it got dark). We couldn't hear what was said, only the rise and fall, the snap of their voices. We prided ourselves on our own lowered tones and hushed exhalations. Not that we had argued once since all that happened at the last flat. Perhaps it was easier not to speak, to not let anything about that night accidentally slip out between other words.

Fence-man didn't seem to enjoy the solitude of his work; he fought the knee-high grass, yanking up handfuls, tossing it to seed another corner. He kept his back hunched, his thin legs bent like each lift of the hammer might break him. He tore, slashed, raged his way through that twenty feet by twenty feet square patch of garden.

Apart from the shouting with the wife, the grunts at the boys, we never saw him speak to anyone. In fact we never saw him anywhere except in that garden. If we ever missed the shouting signal, then the screech of the shed door, the whack of a post, would alert us to his presence. He could break the peaceful watery sunshine of a Sunday afternoon. He could drown out the silence in our maisonette. We were thankful for that.

Whenever Fence-man went out into his garden, he set to work on his fence. Spending a morning banging a post into the earth without bothering to prepare the ground. Smashing at the wood with a hammer or brick. The wife would bring out washing which got left to soak in the rain and stiffen overnight with frost. The sons would come out to call him for dinner, staying long enough to puff a quick fag in the lee of the shed. But no one ever tried to help him with the fence.

Fence-man was always mending: patching with pieces of plastic, buttressing up with old planks he must have dragged in off the street. Only the fence never seemed to get much longer. Sometimes half a side would appear fastened against the wind with sticks and string, but by morning it would be flattening the grass again.

And we knew it meant something, Fence-man and his need to fill the holes, to patch the gaps, but we didn't know what. Or maybe we just couldn't bring ourselves to speak of that Sisyphean task. So, we rolled our eyes instead before drawing the curtains shut on the quick falling blankness of January and its longest nights. Lying, not touching, on either side of the king-size bed, feeling more than a fence separating us.

A new bed was the first thing we bought when we moved in here. And there was always the mortgage to pay, jobs to go to, commutes to compete with, Friday night drinks in pop-up bars (there one night, gone the next), Saturday night dinner parties, slow-cook Sundays – Monday again. And repeat. There was always Fence-man too. Only sometimes, when we closed our eyes, and not always when we were asleep, we dreamed about all that happened in the old flat, about the coloured lantern lights, about the dark blue sheets, about the deep Bordeaux, there had been a lot of that but not enough to blot out what happened next. Sometimes we woke in a tangle of duvet, fists clenched, but other times we woke with watery thighs, a heat inside, the blush of memories on our cheeks. Such heat couldn't keep the winter out.

It was a February storm that chewed up the fencing, all of it, even the two long-standing panels at the rear, battering them all into the weeds.

Fence-man was back the next morning: picking up wood, untangling plastic wiring, bashing and patching. Frost scratched at the fencing, and set in our bones, making us feel old and brittle as the thin wood panels. Fence-man took to pissing in each corner of his garden; we liked to think he was marking his territory, staking claim where even a fence couldn't.

Once we even took a sick day off from our respective offices, sat and watched him from the window. We did feel a little under the weather we told each other, padding the deception with glasses of Berocca and aloe vera coated tissues. But that wasn't to be repeated.

We shivered through spring when heavy rain bloated and rotted the posts. Fence-man banged sharp-pointed stakes into the mud. We tutted in summer when the scrape of Fence-man's handsaw broke through the cheerful banter of our barbeques with friends.

He was an arsehole, intent on ruining everything we did, was what we decided one sweltering July night when the bang of metal on wood seemed to drive up the temperature and sweat splintered on our skin.

Well, it started out as a prank, something to do on the bank holiday. Wouldn't it be funny if one morning, Fence-man got up and found his garden fenced in on all sides? It would be a good deed, like the man in America who helped out his neighbourhood in secret. But the way we laughed turned it into something less than kind. Our chatter that day, each time we discussed it, was sharp and shrill like the screech of magpies in the pines behind Fence-man's garden. The more we spoke of it, the more we staked it out: panels could be got quite cheaply from a garden centre; dark enough in the back gardens, which were out of reach of kitchen and lounge room lights, to sneak between the bushes on our side, creep through the garden between it and Fence-man's patch; such a thing could be done in a few hours even at night, it was all about the planning.

All the talk saved us that long weekend from speaking of the last place, the neighbourliness of the upstairs neighbour. It stopped us from thinking about the pleasant chats over the fence, the winter wine tasting in front of the fire, the way her hair sparked with slivers of red, the small two-seater sofa with its layers of brocade cushions, and it was so hot in that room, and it was late, and we'd drunk at least three bottles of Bordeaux and eaten all the cheese plate, and it was very late, too late to get up and leave, before she (we were sure it was her) asked if we two had ever thought of being a three. We were a two and two is a pair. Three is a crowd the saying goes, and we knew this, as all good clichés are, to be true. But we didn't get up, and we didn't ask her to leave that night. We stayed for far too long.

Back to that bank holiday weekend, already Saturday afternoon, and Homebase didn't shut until eight. We repeated the joke, about erecting the fences, until it wasn't a joke, until we stood at the checkout with six fence panels, twelve posts, a shovel, and a bag of nails. Funny how things can happen when we weren't really thinking, when there wasn't much else to do. Three posts jostling side by side on the belt, fighting for room. Standing there in Homebase, we certainly weren't remembering much of that long-gone night itself, lying panting, a muddle of limbs, watching that third person between us. We weren't really sure how it happened, there were all the pieces, but they weren't in quite the right place. Panels, posts, nails, but not yet a fence. There was the taste of her skin, the slippery glide of a hand between her thighs, the suck and smack of skin...

Will there be anything else? the checkout guy asked. We shook our heads, loaded the trolley again, bumped the wheels out into the car park. Better to think of this new neighbour and his strange infatuation with fencing. He was outside our window, outside us two. Yes, it was a much safer thing to do.

Click, rev, reverse, radio on, back window blocked, boot tied open over the fence panels. We had a good deed to do.

It took a while for it to get dark. It took some time for all the lights to go out. It wasn't like we could get into any trouble; it was a good deed, just a secret one. We took a torch, but really there was enough bright white moonlight to guide us.

Digging holes was harder than we expected. We sweated, we blistered, but we didn't stop. One post, one panel, nails, steadying; a routine that needed concentration and effort. We stopped to look at each other in the moonlight, but we didn't laugh, we didn't even smile. Shadows marked our faces into crumpled angry-looking lines – it was just the cast of the moon that was all. We worked through the night, and we got it done, although we fenced ourselves in and had to scale the left side to get back to our own garden.

We congratulated ourselves before falling asleep clothed in mud and sweat. This would bring us some peace.

Only our gift didn't change anything. Still each day Fenceman appeared. What was his problem? Didn't he have a job other than mending a side of fencing, fencing that no longer needed fixing? A person would have to be wrong in the head to keep working and working at... at nothing.

Each day he would appear, or rather we'd hear him first – shouting at his wife, or yelling at one of his sons, the wisps of his hair waving above the alleyway hedge before he'd surface in his garden. Occasionally now he'd stand in the shed doorway, listening to the cough and crackle of a badly tuned radio, appearing transfixed, staring at the orange wood as it faded under rain and sunshine. Then, that last day he took a hedge trimmer to cut the grass (there weren't any hedges on his patch), uncovering a small fire pit in the middle of the tangle. The swing of the blade sent up dust and weeds, blowing them into neighbouring gardens, sowing seeds of cleavers, nettles, wild geraniums. It wasn't clear how he managed not to slice off his own leg with such grand sweeps, sharp flicks, as he manoeuvred himself around the small square garden.

All done. Fenced, cut, weeded.

We didn't see him for a few weeks after that. It has to be said that we even began to miss his bald head, the wisps of hair, never quite enjoying the silence the way we thought we should. The garden wasn't empty though. The wife would still hang out the washing, only now she started sitting in a deckchair sometimes, her feet up on the bricks, head tilted to the sky. The sons were out there too, smoking in the lee of the shed, lining up beer bottles around the fire pit.

It was the downstairs neighbours who told us that Fenceman had had a heart attack. Hadn't we heard the ambulance screaming into the night? He'd died before he reached the hospital. We slept right through it, but we knew the truth when we heard it. Well, it does, doesn't it? Sometimes the heart just gives out.

And later that summer, not long after we found out, Fenceman's sons had a barbeque in the garden. It went on long long into the baking August night.

We had to sleep with the windows closed, despite the heat, to keep out the smoke and the racket. In the morning, we opened the kitchen blind and saw it. The fence, all down the left side, smouldered. A flame must have got too close, the creosote must have gone up in a flash. A black opening, jagged at the edges.

Nothing seemed to fit together after that; the fire had burned itself into us, the hole couldn't be healed – we had no heart for any of it. Finally, we separated, dividing everything in half, selling the place for less than it was worth. We moved out.

Open House

Standing on the corner of Roman Road, Bethnal Green station behind, Freddie Ierubino recalls his childhood rides on the Underground: scuffed pumps, digging his canvas-covered toes into the ridged boards of the Tube floor; writing his name in the weft of the seat covers but only when his mum wasn't watching. Always the burn of cod liver in his mouth which his mum dosed him with. Its oily taste never quite dislodged by the thick spoonfuls of malt that followed.

The open house is today. He saw the Rightmove listing on the library computer (he was supposed to be searching for one-bedders in Bexleyheath, a warden-controlled future, not searching for the past) but that wasn't why he'd left home. He planned to go to the British Museum to see the new exhibition on Sicily. He'd climbed the station's worn concrete steps, reached the street before he realised where he was. His feet responding to that familiar pattern of his youth even as his knees pulsed with arthritis. This wasn't Bloomsbury; he'd stepped into a museum of memories instead.

Now he is here, there doesn't seem any harm in taking a stroll. He's retired after all; his time is his own. He hasn't been back to Whitechapel since his father's funeral, over twenty years ago. Like the Tube disaster monument, white and angled, don't some things deserve to be remembered? He'll just take a butcher's down Roman Road, go to the British Museum after, and still be back in time for tea.

The concrete and brick around him throb with the unexpected heat of autumn; the sort of day that doesn't know itself. Trees in Bethnal Green Gardens have been fooled into bringing out buds, daffodils peek from the mud, even though it's much too late in the year. London's sky is an apricot haze of tumbled clouds. It reminds Freddie of those walks from the bus stop after a day on the building sites. Summer seemed to last forever back then. Arms swinging, money in his pocket, walking tall like a man, even though he wasn't much more than a boy. His dad always kept a step behind; his heavy gaze weighing Freddie down.

He was fourteen when he first started work, or rather, he was that age when his dad caught him skiving at the back of the flats and marched him down to the building site. Freddie thought he'd take a beating for it, but his dad only put him to work on the lathe, shared his sandwich, bought him a mug of treacly tea off the trolley. It was the first time he heard his dad speaking any English, and Freddie was ashamed for him.

When they got home, Freddie expected his dad to kick the chair out from under him, which was what he did when really raging. But his dad only bashed more brown sauce onto his mash, dosed the sausages with salt. Freddie expected his mum to put the wooden spoon to the back of his legs. But they just sat and ate with only the ticking of the wall clock, the old bloke next door coughing up his lungs, to break the silence at the table.

Freddie put down his fork, said, 'I'm done with school.'

His mum reached over, topped up his mug, replied, 'Dad says you can keep going to work with him.'

Freddie wasn't sure how she always knew what his dad said when he only spoke Italian in the house, and they only spoke English. His mum always acted the interpreter.

A woman in a hijab holds her son's arm, walking along the street, speaking some language Freddie doesn't understand. When his dad was senile, in the home that wasn't his home, and Freddie dressed him, changed his soiled pads, it had made him think for the first time how his dad must have done the same for him once. Or maybe not: his dad was always at work – Monday through to Saturday lunchtime.

Saturday afternoon, his parents would go down the social. The club kept a table for the Italians of the neighbourhood, not to keep them separate but because the men wanted it that way. They laughed and drank, shouted and brawled, and sometimes they sang; no one else knew what the words meant, but the tunes, the crooning, could make you cry.

Sundays his dad would sleep long into the afternoon, waking to make dinner – fish, or pasta, sometimes both. The flat suffused with the smell of oregano, basil, tomatoes, which his dad grew on the balcony. The neighbours had long ago given up complaining about the stink. Accordion music crackled on the gramophone, and when there were no words to be heard above the wheezing notes, the clatter of steaming pots, they were happy together.

A cab blares its horn. A swirl of diesel fumes engulfs Freddie. The mother shakes her son's arm, says something to him. The boy straightens his Spiderman T-shirt, answers, 'I know the way.' She sends him to press the button, makes him wait for the green man before crossing. Freddie follows behind.

Double-deckers and lorries drive close enough to lift the edges of his sports jacket. He tastes grit from all those spinning wheels. That's new, on the left, a Buddhist Centre. No one knew about Buddhists all those years ago, or if they did they never spoke of it. Coming back, time and time again, a circle of life only to be finally completed with enlightenment and release. Freddie knows this because he and Connie went to Thailand in

2002. They took a train to Chiang Mai; Connie wanted to go to a monk chat. He laughed at her, said, What did she want with enlightenment? As he waited for her outside, a yellow-robed monk sat beside him on the bench, rubbing his cracked heels. The monk smiled, said, 'We're always on the path.' Freddie nodded but had no idea what he meant.

His feet lead him on; they have control, and he is the automaton. Following the straight thrust of Roman Road. And there it is – still standing – Ebenezer House. Freddie stares at the red façade, the yellow accent bricks above the windows, which, as a child, made him think the block was smiling. The small green courtyard is well-tended, but iron railings cut if off from the pavement. The kids in the flats used to run down the stairs and straight across the muddy square. Now they'd have to deal with a safety gate first. Freddie runs his hand along the arrow points. Such railings would have been stripped and sold for scrap in his day. But it isn't his day anymore.

A group of youngsters hang around the doorway. Probably about to cause trouble, planning it if not actually doing it. Kids get guns and shoot up places these days or stick blades in each other. But Freddie knows how rage can burn. On his last day at West Street School, he'd wished he had a weapon.

Freddie had held out his hand for the cane, but McElroy pushed him over the bench, beat his backside like he was a snot-nosed junior. Every time McElroy lifted his arm to strike with the cane, he brought his hand down on the desk too. Freddie saw the long ink stain marking the brown sleeve of the geography teacher's jacket, looking like an oxbow river. Freddie had only meant to do it once, dip his pen in the ink and flick, but everyone was sniggering, and Freddie wanted to get a proper laugh. He had dipped the pen again, stretched out his arm, flicked, and as the ink flew through the air, McElroy half turned, chalk in hand. The ink hit his lips and chin, dribbled down his sleeve.

Freddie wanted to pay McElroy out. The memory of that humiliation lived with him, but that was the point: *lived* – he would never have finished the geography teacher off.

A man with a clipboard passes Freddie, heading towards the crowd. He's probably going to shift them or take their names. But on moving closer, although they seemed like kids to Freddie, he realises that they aren't. Some could be nudging thirty. It's hard to tell these days, with the fashion for narrow trousers making them all gangly as newborn foals. These millennials – he's heard them called that on LBC radio – they'd probably laugh to think a father and son couldn't speak the same language; his dad shouting and waving his hands, Freddie answering in English and always trying to speak for his dad on the building sites, anywhere outside the flat. They got by, but never really made themselves understood. He would learn more from that exhibition of Sicily at the museum than he'd ever learned from his dad.

The man with the clipboard does take names, hands out flyers, marshalling everyone into a queue. He lifts the red board above his head, signalling for attention. 'We'll be starting in five minutes. If you haven't given your details, please sign up.' He has a beard, cut low and sharp on his cheeks. He marches up and down the line in his shiny suit like a boy playing at soldiers.

A couple arrives, edging alongside Freddie.

'Here for the open house?' the young man asks.

Freddie looks at the metal-plated door and the row of buzzers for Ebenezer House. He nods. Freddie isn't a man to believe in fate, but coincidences have their own rhythm. He steps into the line. The young man tuts, mutters something to the woman with him. She replies with a hot and flustered, 'How was I supposed to know there'd be so many?'

The estate agent reaches Freddie, grips a pen. He isn't quick enough to think up a lie, and gives his name: 'Ierubino, Freddie.'

Saying it out loud makes him flinch, expecting someone to repeat it back to him and say, 'What an age it's been.' No one does, of course. It's been too long. The only echo he hears (and it's just inside his head) is his mum's voice, slapping against bricks, bouncing about the courtyard like a pumped-up football: 'Freddie Ierubino, get in for your tea.'

There must be about twenty in the queue, including the young couple behind him. They all look like they've come from a day at the park: running shoes, backpacks. There's even a girl with a wide-brimmed straw hat like the one Connie took to keep the sun out of her eyes in Thailand. When Freddie was growing up in the third-floor flat, looking out on black tarmac and yellow streetlamps, he never imagined he'd one day take a guided tour of golden-domed temples in Bangkok, or crest waves in a dragon-painted boat along the shores of Phuket. And when he left the house this morning, he never thought he'd end up at these flats. Funny how things turn out.

The estate agent punches numbers into the keypad, leans back, levering the heavy door. Freddie follows the people inside. It will make a good story to tell Connie. When he gets home, after putting the kettle on, cracking open the biscuit barrel, picking out a rich tea, he will say to her, 'You'll never guess where I went today.' She might say, 'Oh, Freddie. What you gone and done now?' Only she won't, of course. She's been gone these past five months.

The girl in the hat holding hands with the girl who's dressed like a boy, in oversize shirt and black boots, three places up in the queue, she has a look of Connie. He supposes them to be lesbians. He's long thought women must be a separate species, and the idea of them living, breeding, succeeding together gives him a sense of tingling excitement that his sort might just die out one day. The last of the line; he wouldn't mind that on his gravestone. But anything he wants engraved, he'll have to leave in writing with Pew the solicitor; he and Connie never had any children. Nieces and nephews, godchildren, had all dropped off the Christmas-card list over the years. But plenty of other people think they get a say in his future. The doctors said he should carry an alarm in case of falls, the lady from the council arranged meals-on-wheels, the neighbour on the left talked of all the space he had in the house and wouldn't he be better in a nice small flat?

On the first landing, from behind cracked glass, a noticeboard advertises a drop-in centre, a diabetes surgery, and a housing meeting to be held next week. Freddie's got his Freedom Pass, his British Museum Member's pass; he doesn't need anything else. He's going to sell up the house, his and Connie's place, and buy himself a small flat closer to the shops – he supposes the busybodies have a point. He has a whole list of things to keep him occupied. He certainly won't be joining any residents committee.

A committee should get these hallways redecorated. The floor is painted with a rubbery grey substance that will probably take thousands of years to rot away, but some yob has tried to speed things up, burned a hole in the middle of it. Freddie steps around the black bubbles, fossilised mid burst.

On the narrow turn between the landings, Freddie realises his coming back here is a mistake. What was he thinking, digging around in the past? It's all over and done with.

For once Freddie knows he should do what he planned to do – go to the British Museum, inspect history from behind polished glass.

He tries to turn and go back down the stairs, but the young couple behind him are too busy to notice. Heads held close, peering at a phone like it is a mirror. He'll have to push between them to get downstairs, and what if the door needs an exit code? What if he's stuck until someone comes by?

There's not enough air down there. No choice but to keep going higher. Past the second floor. They stop at the third. His old floor. All the doors are painted red. Were they always that colour? His hand must have pressed against the paint, pushed his way in, so many times, but he can't recall – blue, maybe.

The estate agent has trouble holding them back; the queue spills into the flat. Freddie feels a jolt of anticipation, peeking through the doorway. He steps inside. The young couple bangs into him, but he doesn't move. They mutter something – apology or insult, Freddie isn't sure which. He steadies himself against the wall. He might as well be stood in some flat in some other city, some other country. Nothing is as it was.

An antique coat-stand is rooted in the narrow hall. Floorboards brightly varnished as if they're something to be proud of. His mum saved for over a year to get harlequin lino laid. Words are framed on the walls, enough to make his vision blur: *Love; Home Sweet Home;* something foreign about a pipe.

Freddie shakes his head. He is an old fool, but part of him expected his mum's checked housecoat to flash by the kitchen door, the racing results to trot out from the front-room radio, the sweet muskiness of fried liver and onions to greet him.

The estate agent pops in and out of rooms, wafting a smell of aftershave and mints, offering up measurements and dimensions as if giving benedictions. Freddie loosens his top button. There are too many people. They make polite elbow room like visitors at a stately home.

The girlfriends – or maybe they're married, that's allowed these days – loiter in the hall, checking each room from the threshold without entering. The one with the hat fans herself with the wide brim. Connie always liked young people, watching them with the same joy she had when *You've Been Framed* came on (although she never laughed when it seemed the man falling off the skis or the woman toppling off the boat might have actually hurt themselves). Connie collected sunglasses and jewellery like a magpie; if she saw it in a magazine, she wanted it. Nothing expensive, mind, just brightly coloured enough to make her ask, 'Does it make me look twenty years younger?' Freddie wishes now, with all his heart, he'd said 'Yes' just once.

He feels an attachment to those girls, not because the pretty one has the same hazel eyes, the same square jaw as Connie. No, it's something else. He bets they never do anything without meaning to; they look the type to plan things and think that planning makes it bound to happen. He won't be the one to tell them otherwise.

He smiles at the boyish girl, and she gives him a nod that says, 'I see you'. No one has seen Freddie for some time. There's no one to remember him as anything but old, and maybe it was selfish to hope he'd be the first to go. What with Connie's Grape-Nuts, cottage cheese and Ryvita-eating ways, she should have long outlived him.

Now Freddie knows he'll be the last to leave, probably left in a shared room of a council-run facility, where the staff will be nice but young, so young. One day they'll forget he has trouble eating dry food because of his acid reflux, they'll offer him a digestive and he'll take it because he won't remember he shouldn't, and he'll choke right there in his single bed; biscuit crumbs and vomit.

What a self-pitying fool!

Freddie rubs the stubble on his chin. He didn't shave this morning; everything knocked off the axis that was his usual routine with Connie gone. That was one of Freddie's last memories of this flat: loss striking his dad with such force he never quite stood straight again.

Freddie will never forget how his dad cried when the phone fell out of his hand. It hit the lino in the hallway, cracked it in two. On looking closely now, Freddie sees the crack went down to the floorboards, although they hadn't known that back then.

He places his foot over the split in the wood. The young couple put their palms on the walls as if they can measure the thickness that way. They point out coving, which never used to be there, and coo quietly (so the estate agent won't hear) about 'original features'.

It had been an original sight to see his dad cry. Freddie hadn't been sure what to do. He raised his arm a little to offer some comfort, but the thought of touching his dad after all those years of taking care not to even brush elbows on visits home, made his limb too heavy to lift. His dad's sobs became wails; the sort he'd seen on the news from widows in Kuwait, tearing at their black robes, trying to shred the pain from their bodies. Freddie kept his arms at his sides, went into the kitchen, set the kettle on the hob. He stood close to the gas ring, waiting for the whistling steam to smother the sound. He hadn't meant to ignore his dad's tears, but there didn't seem to be anything else to be done.

Now Freddie stands in the kitchen doorway again, that memory stops him from entering. A girl with pink hair, and a bolt through her left ear, peers out the window onto the netted balcony. It's all changed, of course. Shiny-white melamine countertops and cupboards. A pot of sugar left on the side. Flies will lay eggs in it. A browning copy of *Metro* sits on top of a recycling box. A calendar by the microwave is two weeks out of date. It's as if the owners have vanished. Freddie has read stories about that in the *Daily Mail*, people walking out on their families, their lives. What would make a person do that?

His mum always said, 'A place for everything and everything in its place.' She was the sort of woman who could often be found with the cupboards open, bottles of brown sauce, malt vinegar, tinned tapioca lined up on newspaper laid out on the kitchen floor as she scrubbed the inside shelves. With a surgeon's precision, she'd slide the cloth, soaked with white spirit and lemon juice, into each corner, carefully nipping off smears with a dry duster. She never would have left an old paper on the side, uncovered sugar, or an out-of-date calendar on the wall. Every time they went on their week's holiday to the Isle of Wight, before they left, his mum always set the calendar forward to the date of their return. He used to think it was because she took pride in being organised, but maybe there was a touch of superstition about it too – willing them all into a future together.

Freddie waited all year for those summer trips. The taste of salt on his skin, crackling sand in his socks. Fish and chips on the rocks, throwing batter bits to acrobatic gulls. Waving to the passing ferry, thankful that his turn to leave hadn't yet come.

He feels now that he's the only one left on the shore, waving and waving, watching everything that was his life sailing across the Solent. But his turn will come.

Freddie heads for the bathroom. He wouldn't mind taking a moment for himself, running his hands under cold water, rubbing his eyes. But the bathroom holds a crowd. Freddie doesn't like the press of shoulders and backs, making him a spectator of the avocado three-piece bathroom set. Someone has tried to bring that 1970s choice of his mum's up to date with palm-print wallpaper and fancy silver light fittings. Someone has tried to mask the flowered tiles with paint, but it flakes and cracks in patches. It looks about as ugly as Freddie could imagine. Someone laughs. He moves away, feeling guilty for being part of that judgement on his mum's taste.

Freddie picks at the chipped blue paint on the wall of his old bedroom. These flats were built to last; that 1950s vision was meant to see them through to the space age. Living on the moon, a phosphorus-bright world high in the sky. It hadn't quite happened that way. Connie became his home. Over the years they grew into each other like ivy burrows into the cracks of a wall. There could be no pulling them apart without the pointing crumbling, the structure failing. But here he is – still standing. How can that be?

Freddie looks around. The girls have gone; the pink-haired one isn't anywhere to be seen. He didn't notice any of them leave. The couple who'd stood behind him in the queue is still there, opening wardrobes as if the contents are for sale too.

The estate agent chews on the end of his pen, staring out the window, probably imagining himself selling a penthouse with a WC1 postcode. He glances up. Freddie sidesteps him into the front room. His mum would have approved of how they have done it out: like a country cottage, all white wood and pink roses. The floor slopes a little before reaching the skirting. Freddie stands in the dip. His mum used to keep her armchair by the window too, although she always complained about the draught.

It was pneumonia that finally did for her. 'Don't let me die alone,' is what she made them promise at the hospital. He told her they'd be right back.

Freddie had persuaded his dad to go home for a bath and a change. It was embarrassing sitting next to him on the plastic bedside chairs – mustard stains on his jumper, dandruff on his shoulders. They heard the phone ringing before they even put the key in the lock. His dad held the receiver away from his ear so Freddie could hear. 'She's gone,' the voice said. And his father, who often made out he couldn't understand a word of English, knew exactly what the nurse meant. He dropped the phone to the floor.

Freddie hears the front door open, voices in the hallway. Perhaps they will just forget he is here. He is good at silence these days.

The estate agent is talking, seeing off the last of them. He will come for Freddie next.

Clipboard clutched to his chest he fills the threshold, shrugs his shoulders at Freddie. 'It's sealed bids. We've already had offers. But go away, think about it if you like.'

Who is he to say 'go away'? Who is he to say anything?

Freddie thrusts out his hands. 'Go on, clear off!'

His palms slip on the estate agent's shiny suit. Freddie shoves again, driving him towards the front door. Freddie hates him. Hates those polished fingernails, the too heavy silver watch. He is old, but the estate agent doesn't see this coming. Freddie has the advantage at last. He gets him out the door. Deadlocks the bolt. Barricades it with his back. Knees bending, sinking to the floor.

Finally the banging had stopped, and the estate agent went from shouting to muttering something into a phone. Freddie certainly wasn't going to open the door to him. He had time to think at least, think about what the day should have been. What it all should have been.

A policewoman arrived with a gentle tapping on the door, a calmness to her voice.

She is still here, calling to him again, 'We need to know you're all right.'

Freddie knows he should tell her, 'There's nothing wrong with me.' And there isn't. But a person's life shouldn't be an open house, for strangers to trample through and pick over, not even knowing what they are looking at, as if someone's removed every label from the British Museum, leaving tourists to guess meaning from those fragments of the past.

From where Freddie sits, he sees small planes coming in to land at City airport, mammoth-bellied Boeings rising high after take-off from Heathrow. He should like to go back to Thailand, find that monk, ask him, 'Where is the path?' He turns. The policewoman's lips and nose are visible through the letter flap. Maybe he could whisper it through that thin metal gap, letting all the things he ever wanted to say slip out. He puts his hand over his mouth.

He wants to return. He wants to feel the warmth of his mum's hug as he comes through the door, her housecoat, flapping about him; he wants to taste the sweetness of his dad's balcony-grown tomatoes, smell them simmering for hours; he wants to fall asleep in Connie's arms, wake and see her smiling face again. He just can't see the way.

How can he tell the policewoman any of that? He's never had the words, and she is too young to know that life can leave you with only memories, not the touch of skin, the heaviness of a slap, the tingling of a lover's pinch. He places his palm over the crack in the floorboards and knows when his time comes there will be nobody left to speak his name, no one waiting for that call. He holds up his hands – empty. Between his fingers, more planes cut across the sky.

Life has a way of flying away, leaving you dispersed, insubstantial as vapour trail, and there isn't any way to gather all those tiny particle pieces together again.

Shoots and Weeds

Remember me when I am gone away. So says the engraved bench on the left. The gardener hasn't got time for that today. He starts the motor; it splutters gas, sneezing out leaves and dust.

Bang. The wheels bite down on tarmac. He revs, gets nowhere, stranded half on the grass, half on the path. A sea of suits, sipping from paper cups, eyes to phones, wander in front of him. He swerves around them. He's not even a ripple in their day.

The engine sputters to a halt beside a bin. He gets off, checks under the blades. A shredded copy of yesterday's *Metro* falls apart like confetti. He slaps his hands clean. Wouldn't life be easier without people? Sandwich packets, drink cans, condoms, one time he even found... but no, his stomach turns to think of it this early in the day.

Leave the garden to the trees and the squirrels, is what he thinks. But no one's going to ask him for his thoughts. He eases himself into the seat, zips up his fleece against the autumn chill. The ignition bites, the motor rumbles, but the path ahead is blocked. A tourist takes a selfie. The gardener leans out of the way.

That's what he calls himself, a gardener, not a council amenity maintenance worker like the contract says. No maintenance worker ever eased a daffodil bud from cracked frost or mulched leaves to blanket roses. He tends Russell Square Gardens like it is his own. And really it is, certainly hasn't got anything else to call his own: no home, no wife; even the kids he only gets to see between eleven and four thirty on a Sunday.

Now the boss is beckoning him over, bald head glistening. He probably wants the gardener to help with the leaves. There's still grass to cut over by the fountain, but what choice does the gardener have?

Gears crunching, he manoeuvres the trailer up to the waiting flatbed. The boss pretends to wave him in like he controls the wheels on the gardener's motor. He'd love to lift his foot off the brake, zoom backwards, trapping the boss against the flatbed, breaking him in two, but he doesn't. He backs up slowly: showing his arse like a chained-up bitch to the dog. The boss comes over. 'When you're finished, there's weeding to be done, over by the gates.'

The gardener nods, but he won't do it. The boss likes everyone to think the Gardens run to his rules, but he wouldn't know a green shoot from a weed. The gardener planted those cyclamens himself; the buds are just peaking out. The boss thinks all unwanted plants are weeds. The gardener dumps the grass cuttings. An avalanche tumbles over the flatbed onto the boss' boots. Now the old git will have to do some work.

He speeds off across the grass. Which should be a number two cut like the barber gives. But the boss only cares about his mortgage and his pension. Parks aren't what they used to be, the boss said once, shaking his head as if it wasn't his fault spending all the budget on the cafe and fountain. Plants are what they always are, with love and attention anyway, and the gardener does his best to keep them that way.

It's the last thing the gardener's wife said to him, You're not what you used to be. Not long after that, she became his ex-wife – like a spade through him and her, signed papers, turned over all those years together. He drives under the bare yews. Cut down a tree, and you'll still see its stump; dig up the roots, lay new turf, more than likely a ring of mushrooms will appear to show where it stood. Some things are forever.

He breathes in the burn of petrol, the grease of pizza from the cafe. Inside, sealed off behind glass, people mouth words to each other. Does anyone ever really know what's being said? The gardener doesn't need to listen to them; he would rather put his ear to the flowerbeds and listen to the squeak of new shoots cresting through the mud.

His ex-wife used to say to him, Are you deaf?

But he's not. All morning he hears blackbirds chatter, squirrels squeal, the holm oaks creak. He listens hard so he doesn't have to hear the other things in his head. The boss tells him to wear earplugs.

Health and Safety can go to hell.

Nothing drowns out the rush of blood in his ears. Not even the cries of his oldest, Poppy, when he drops her back at her mum's after Sundays spent catching her from slides. Soon she'll be old enough to notice how he squeezes her too tight, how his eyes mist when he waves goodbye – soon she'll grow to hate him for it, but if he's lucky eventually it might turn to pity. These are the thoughts he leaves buried in the leaf piles; the ones he burns in the barrel and spreads back over the flowerbeds.

The lunchtime crowd is out. A suit sits in the middle of the gardener's patch, digging in headphones like he doesn't notice the motor. The gardener bleeds the fuel line, smokes him out of there. See him go!

The gardener's wife ran off too. But he's the one in digs so small that from his bed he can open the fridge with his foot. He wouldn't take the kids to that bedsit. Not that his wife will let him have little Michael overnight. As if the gardener doesn't know how to soothe and tuck-in a baby after years of bedding chrysanthemums.

He parks the motor on the path, takes his sausage roll and Lilt to the bench under the hollies. Sun drips through the prickly leaves, shaping the shadows into icicles. No peace lasts long. A woman in tight jeans and a fluffy cardigan sits down on the other end of the bench. She's got the grace of a dancer, thick calf muscles too. She opens up a Spa bag full of tin foil packages. He feels her staring at him, probably thinks the benches are only for visitors.

She points at him. 'A taste of tropical paradise.'

He frowns, then he gets it – she's pointing at the can. 'Who couldn't do with an escape?'

She holds up her hand, wide as a trowel. 'Me, for one.'

He licks pastry from his fingers. She's not so young this woman, there's a hardness to her face like frost around the edges, but she's got a smile that makes him feel like a bit of orange autumn light has settled on the bench.

She offers a cigarette. He hasn't smoked for years. It stains the wallpaper, his wife used to say.

He sucks deep, fills his lungs with the sharp heat. The sun dips. He stretches out, taking his last chance at it; rubs his hand over the mossy plaque: *Remember me when I am gone away.* What he'd like written, a message for his kids, there's not enough room on any bench to inscribe: *Tried my best. Got it wrong, course I did. But I love you – try to forgive me the rest.*

'I love this spot,' she says.

Some might think her a sad cow for having nothing better to love – not the gardener. He smiles.

She holds up a tin foil parcel of raisins; she's missing the tip of the little finger on her right hand. He nods, takes what she offers. And really it's what he's always hoped for: that come the end of the season, someone recognises him as a shoot, not a weed.

The Jam Trap

I was eighteen when I found out what sort of man I was to be. I thought I was going to be a hard-working, big-earning, sort of man. I'd have a wife, a couple of kids, and probably a spaniel. But that was before I took that summer job at the Beach Cafe on Ryde seafront.

I can still see the blue awning and white plastic chairs from this bench opposite the boating lake where I'm sat. Some things don't change, and that's the way I like it. Facebook, Twitter, Vine, Snapchat – constant variety, from governments to lattes, scrolling on and on – such things make my head ache and my neck itch. That's why I like this bench, sitting here (on the far left), watching the tide which I know will come in and go out because it has every day I've been here, and so I presume will continue to do so. But I wasn't always this still. Once, I was eighteen and eager to be on the other side of that water, setting off on my big mainland adventure. If you don't know it already, 'mainland' is what Island people call the rest of it over there. And before I could leave, I needed one last summer job to wait out the exam results and fill my wallet. I picked the Beach Cafe as it was right on the seafront, Appley Sands rippling out in front. I wanted a view over the Solent because it was to be my last summer before going off to uni. Maybe I had some inkling of it even then, that I wasn't ready to leave, but I can't be sure of that.

I turned up at the Beach Cafe one lunchtime when the sun was out, and the queues were long. I got the job because I was skinny enough to fit the only spare T-shirt they had left. Pale blue, scratchy cotton, a yellow beach and green palm tree emblem stitched just above my heart.

I wasn't wrong about the view from the cafe. My first day working in the kitchen, side door propped open to let in a breeze and let out the wasps, I heard the lap of waves, the rustle of sand. From the Mr Whippy machine on the front counter, I watched the catamaran cut through the water to Portsmouth Harbour. The mainland – that's where I was going. The rippled sandbars stretched so far out it almost felt like you could walk over to the other side; you couldn't of course and that's why what happened was just waiting to happen, like an upturned hull emerging from the silt at low tide; the right winds, the turn of the current and after years submerged it would appear.

Usually there was me and one of the girls working the counter and kitchen between us. The toaster popped charred teacakes, piled and waiting to be scraped. The fryers crackled with starch, spitting chips to the oily surface; scampi curled and crisped; trays of cakes arrived each Wednesday – we weren't allowed to eat them.

The owner, Mrs Tudor, did the cooking. She liked to keep note of everything that left the kitchen, adding it to the spreadsheet in her head. She made us each a sandwich for our lunch break, but you could tell she didn't really want to; only had to lift the drying bread, see only one buttered side, to know profit and loss was her thing. She even hated the wasps, probably thought they were stealing her sugar, driving off her customers. So she kept a jar on the windowsill, half full of watered-down jam; let the sun heat it, let it lure the wasps to a sticky drowning death.

The only thing she didn't make was the tray of glossy iced slices of cake that arrived every Wednesday. I remember the first time I saw them, wide slabs of toffee and coffee coloured icing feathered with white stripes. Mrs Tudor lifted them out one by one, stacking them on the cake stands, sealing them under glass domes to keep off the wasps.

I must have been standing too close as she knocked an elbow into my chest.

She said, 'Stand back, can't afford to drop one of these.'

The cakes were off limits, that much was clear. But I wanted one. She edged back. I pressed myself against the fridge. She carried the loaded cake stand out in front as if even breath might damage them. With her out of the kitchen, I slid my thumb around the edge of the plastic tray they came in. The icing was sweet and salty, melting on my tongue. I wanted more, but Mrs Tudor was always hovering.

She was there every day, but on weekends the Beach Cafe stayed open late. It caught the Balcony Bar nightclub crowd, those back from a day trip spent at the big shops in Portsmouth, and those laying down ballast for a night of drinking at The King Lud. On those weekend nights, her husband was in charge – or so she must have thought.

I worked those weekend evenings because I needed the money. But also because the only other thing to do was hit the Balcony Bar: thrash to Rage Against the Machine and anything by Nirvana; wake up Sunday lunchtime, head stiff on the pillow and have to use my hand to lift my chin; stay in pyjamas until Monday morning.

Those weekend shifts were different from the daytime chores of holidaymakers, pensioners, and small kids cradling sticky pennies. Mr Tudor didn't care if we cooked too many chips and ate the leftovers straight from the dripping fry basket. Mr Tudor didn't care if we gave our drunk mates Mr Whippy packed down to the bottom of the cone.

Mr Tudor didn't care about anything but the card circle he ran on Fridays from the kitchen. Mr Ali, Den the Fish, and Mr

Tudor. A bottle of Bells stood as the centrepiece to that still life. Between games they might try to corner one of the girls against the fridge, getting nothing but an elbow in the ribs for their troubles. Sometimes they'd pour a shot for me, straight into a teacup, and I'd down it between serving customers. If I was gone too long, they'd call me back into the kitchen on some pretence; usually to fill up the jam trap on the windowsill – even at night, the wasps were drawn by the lights and the smell. The men took it in turns to utter helpful comments as I worked.

'Take it up the front, lad.'

'Give it a poke.'

'Not too hard now, boy.'

'Gently does it.'

They spoke to each other really, not me, nudging, winking. None of them was getting any; I'd heard them talking about it before. Mr Ali's wife had three children, a job with an accountant's office in Newport, which all came before he did. Den the Fish lost his wife to a heart attack five years back, and no matter how many Bacardi Breezers he bought for girls at the Balcony nightclub, he wasn't getting any sweetness in return. Mr Tudor never spoke about it, but he couldn't be getting any either. His wife ran the Beach Cafe in a foaming cloud of umbrage and sharp remarks; she saved her tight smiles for the customers.

'Never get married, lad. It's a headache—'

'Ball ache—'

'Bitch ache more like.'

In some ways, I have the Beach Cafe and those card-playing men to thank for offering up a warning about life. What I have now isn't bad, but it isn't what I thought it would be – university, marriage, kids, a spaniel. There's some peace in finding out at such a young age how your life will unfold – no false hope, no shattered dreams. I still keep a jam trap on my windowsill.

Sometimes I sit and watch a wasp drown in sweetness and lust. At such times, I can say to myself, 'I'm happy with my lot.'

I shift on the bench. Sand sticks to my lips, crunching between my teeth. The tide is turning, waves rolling back up the beach. I will keep returning to this spot, and I suppose that will always be the way of things until my tomorrows are all used up, no more cards in the pack. It's getting close to sunset. The wind shifts slightly, moving to touch the other side of my face. I come here most evenings to watch the receding day. It always makes me think of that last day at the Beach Cafe; I was supposed to pick up my A-Level results the week after, but as it turned out, I never did.

That last day at the cafe was a Wednesday, cake delivery day. The tray of cakes was delivered late, nearly evening. Mrs Tudor was busy with the drinks-display repairman. The middle of summer wasn't the time to be without refrigerated fizzy drinks. She left me to receive the delivery and clean up in the kitchen.

The cake tray was heavy in my arms. I staggered from the side door to the prep-station in the middle of the room. A wasp landed on a slice, sinking into the icing. It freed itself, buzzed over to the window only to crawl into the jam trap on the sill. The slice couldn't be sold, not that the wasp had done any real damage, but it wouldn't be hygienic, would it?

I took a step out of the kitchen; there was a queue at the counter, and Mrs Tudor was banging the side of the drink cabinet as the repairman made notes in his book. I didn't want to draw her attention now; she'd be on my case about bleaching the counters properly. I went back into the kitchen, slid out the not so damaged piece of cake. I took it over to the window, where, if someone peaked in from the cafe, they wouldn't be able to see past the freezer, wouldn't be able to see me eating the sweet slice.

Wasps buzzed and thrashed in the jam trap on the sill.

Most of the holidaymakers had gone home or headed back to the high street with its pubs and chip shops. But there was one family still playing on the exposed sand. The tide was right out, and the sun was a burning orange ball balanced above the thin strip of sea in the distance. Back in school, we had studied paintings by Lowry, and that's what they looked like out on the beach. Black stick figures, mother, father, young son, hands raised to eyes, sea spray dusting the air, dwarfed by the bright white liners cruising into Portsmouth docks.

I took a bite of the cake. The icing melted on my tongue, but the sponge was chilled, making it taste stale. It stuck to the roof of my mouth.

Standing by the window.

Drone of wasps drowning in watery jam.

The boy digging, tipping sand into a green bucket.

The tide turned.

He was standing on a sandbar, then he wasn't.

Green beach bucket in the water, bobbing in the waves.

The sky turned red.

Water glinted.

Tide ran in fast.

Hovercraft breaking waves in the distance.

How far out was the boy?

I dropped the half-eaten cake onto the windowsill beside the jam trap. I stepped out of the door. Ran across the grass.

I heard Mrs Tudor through the open kitchen door. 'Who took this cake?'

The little boy was cut off by the tide. I wasn't the only one to see him. The mother was running too, waist-deep into the water. A dog walker from the esplanade ran to the lifeboat station. The father overtook the mother; up to his neck before he surfaced on the last dot of the sandbar.

The bucket washed out to sea. The little boy rode back to the beach on his father's shoulders, into the waiting beach towel held open by his mother.

That's when I saw it – what no one else could see. I knew they couldn't see it because they all watched the boy, his mother hugging him closer than close. But even if one of them had glanced up, all they would have seen is the sunset. Red, orange, sinking into the darkening sea. That's not what I saw.

I had to sit down on the bench (the one I visit every day now). My head dizzy with it. Gripping the peeling wooden slats, to have something to keep me steady, to stop me sliding off the world.

The cake never got eaten, and I never owned up, and no one cared to ask more after all that happened that evening. I saw Mrs Tudor swipe the slice into the bin, and when her kids arrived later, she held them close, they squirmed and tried to pull away, but she held on.

I didn't pick up those exam results; some things are best not to know, to fuel the what-ifs. It wasn't to be. I keep an eye on this place, the sea, these holidaymakers – it's enough. The mainland's not for me. That's why I've come to this bench as often as I could for many years now, to wait out the end of each day.

Sunset – it's a word with meaning, but it's not the truth of this island or the mainland. It's not the sun sinking. It's the earth rolling backwards. Continually moving. I saw it, saw the earth, myself, toppling backwards, losing my place on this small island, sinking somewhere out there on the mainland. It took all my strength just to hold on. Nothing is what it seems, and we don't know how to look for what's really there. It's all a jam trap – wasps enjoying their own demise. I'm not saying that's wrong. I'm just saying there's no reason for me to leave this spot. No need for me to go looking for something that doesn't exist. This is where I belong.

Somebody Said

Somebody said if you wanted to buy grass in London, you should go to Hyde Park. I know, sounds like a joke doesn't it? But we were only fifteen, what did we know?

So, we got off the school coach, and while the rest of them traipsed over to the Tate, we got on a red bus and headed to Hyde Park. We... well, I'm going to use her real name because maybe she'll read this, and if she doesn't, maybe someone who knows her will. But I'm not going to tell you my name – that's cowardly, isn't it? It doesn't matter; you're going to think worse things of me by the time this is through.

We... Kat and me sat on the top deck. We emptied our purses and pockets; didn't have much more than three lip balms, a couple of hairbands, and four quid between us. I don't suppose we stopped to think how it wouldn't be enough. Laughing, we put our feet up on the bar of the seat in front, tilted back our heads, following the sun like daisies. The city was a grey haze outside the windows. Little cars, smaller people. We towered above London's streets, which is probably the only reason I didn't bite my lips, use up the cherry balm, worrying away at myself. I'd never much been outside of our small home town.

Kat slid out of her blue school jumper, draped it around her neck. I did the same. It was soupy and warm up on the top deck. I closed my eyes, breathing in the diesel fumes, the stink of sweat, sweet notes of Impulse body spray. It smelled good, like life – not the blank saltiness of our town and its grey sea views. I could have stayed on that bus all day; shaken into a waking dream in which I saw all that our life could be – me and Kat living in London, far from home and all that home was.

Kat tapped my arm, climbed over me, pulling me to the stairs. I don't know how I'd missed it, but Hyde Park was right there beside the bus. We rushed down the narrow stairs, out onto the street. We had over four hours before we were due back on the coach. No one was going to miss us. The park was wide and open, and comfortably still after so much city speeding past the bus windows. Kat led the way, she usually did, and we left the heat of the tarmac path; heading for the shade of the trees, the depth of the bushes.

That somebody spoke the truth (about the grass that is). It's easier than you'd think to get booze and smokes for free when you're a teenage girl, especially when you're wearing school uniform. And there wasn't any harm in it. Those three men with sleeping bags at their sides, and rucksacks full of what was left of their lives, they couldn't hurt us. They knew it too. Girls like Kat didn't sit down with drunks in parks unless they were already bruised around the edges. I sat beside Kat, took a hit when it was passed, took a swig when it came my way. It all came from Kat's hand. Her thin fingers coloured green at the base, missing all her usual metal rings – jewellery wasn't allowed at school, only a cross, and stud earrings. Nothing much was allowed at Christ Our Saviour – and He wasn't as it turns out, not in this story anyway.

Hot and lightheaded. I leaned over, draped my arm around Kat, kissed her on the cheek. The men sniggered. Kat smiled, said, We're good as sisters. The men sniggered more until lager foamed out of their nostrils.

Good as sisters. Oh, Kat, mine was a low-down Judas kiss. But:

I was fifteen.

I was high.

I was wanting to be so many things.

Of course we shared more than just those sun soaked-hours on the burnt lawns of Hyde Park. But I have no right to claim I know what Kat went through. I found my way back after all, because I had somewhere safe to go. Kat was the danger for me. I loved her, and I hurt her; I don't suppose she ever expected anything else. Don't worry, I'm not saying that to clear myself of any blame. I'm only saying it because it was true.

Really, the park, the drunks, that hot hot day, all that is the end of this story, or near to the end, near to an end as it can ever get – it will never be the final end not until I'm gone too. But I've started now...

Somebody said, Take another hit.

I shook my head. Hyde Park, the trees, the grass, all of it swallowed me up. Felt like I was sinking deep into the cracks of the dried-out mud.

Kat said, Lie down, put your head on my lap.

When I finally woke up, I thought I was dead, or buried in a shallow grave, cast over with mud. No breath to scream. After a moment, the orange pools of streetlights came into focus. The roar of traffic separated from the thudding of the hangover inside my head. I sat up.

I was alone.

Only a scattering of Tennent's cans, and damp roach ends, picked out like stars in the blackness around me, to show that I hadn't started out on my own. I stumbled onto the path, didn't even look for Kat, never even called her name. Walked and walked.

By the time I found the policewoman, I was crying like a small child. I said, I'm lost. My friend is lost too, but she doesn't want to find her way back – not yet.

And there are gaps in all of this, time that slipped past that I have no memory of. That's what makes it hard to tell this story, because it's not a story. There are only snapshots left, fast fading and curled at the edges. I'm not what anyone would call a reliable witness. The dark park. The policewoman with brown scraped-back hair and chapped lips. Then other things must have happened, but I remember nothing else until I was sat back on the coach.

Sat back on the school coach and the journey took a lifetime.

Somebody said, Why would Kat run away?

Somebody said, What was Kat doing with those men?

I said nothing. What I should have done was screamed out, You know what and why! You'd have to be dumb not to guess it. Tell me you know those things, and I'll tell you *who*. But no one has ever asked me that.

I said nothing, stared out of the coach window, hoping to melt into the streaks of yellow motorway light. But each thump of the tyres, each jolt in the road, beat the words into me: *Kat's never coming back. Never coming back.*

Girls don't just lose themselves in parks, in cities, not even one's as big as Hyde Park. But it can be done – it's a bit like the opposite of *Wizard of Oz*, you know that yellow brick road, because there aren't any yellow bricks to follow for one, and for two it was more like bricks have been dug up, tossed into the high grass, rolled into a river, until you look down and see there are no bricks, no path, nothing. And then, well it's the easiest thing in the world to lose your way. That's how it was for Kat. I suppose there was enough path for me. Lucky lucky me. What I've never been able to get out of my thoughts is that I headed straight for my path and never looked back.

I let Kat disappear.

I see her fingers in my dreams sometimes, the cheap silvery rings that left green lines on her skin, the bitten down nails, the picked off glitter polish. I feel her stroking my head, a little too hard, as if she's trying to get in under my skin, into my brain, to find some shelter there.

It's not that I think of her all the time, not all these years later. But sometimes, there'll be a young face at a bus window that will stop me, or the musky scent of flowers will bring her back, but she's always fifteen years old even these fifteen years later. I don't try to summon her; I don't try to cause myself more pain, but I still smoke grass, even now I'm in my thirties, at least I tell myself it is grass. My throat tells me its skunk – which isn't exactly organic, definitely not fair-trade – sometimes I just need to trim the edges off – yes, I know there are drug gangs, and county line kids, and all that – but then, I never learn – didn't I tell you you'd think worse things of me? What did I do but fall asleep in a park, wake up on my own? I really did so much more, or didn't do so many things before that day of the school trip had even started.

I can't say when it started for Kat, and I only know what I saw. Sometimes I don't even know if that's true. Maybe I didn't see... didn't hear... didn't feel...

Let's just say some of this happened, and maybe some of it didn't, but all of it is true.

So, I'll try to tell it again. Properly this time. From the beginning, from the beginning of me and her.

Back in middle school, I had this friend... Kat.

So, Kat had these green almond-shaped eyes that didn't belong on a girl so young. If you stood a step behind her, you might think she watched you, so widely spaced were her pupils. She was too old for baby teeth, but that's what filled her mouth.

Kat chatted and giggled through break-times, always surrounded by girls with pretty T-bar sandals and badges pinned to their flowery rucksacks. I had a grey briefcase which I picked myself from the sale shelf at Woolworths.

I was excited when she asked me to her house. She said it was my turn. At the time I didn't know what that meant. The other girls smiled at me once Kat made the offer. They made space for me at the lunch tables. They waved at me from the school bus. They played with the spinning combination on my briefcase. It was as if I'd pulled out of that case everything I'd ever wanted from school.

When the Saturday of the sleepover came, my mum helped me pack a Spar carrier bag with clean knickers, socks, toothbrush and paste – strawberry flavoured for kids. Even now, I hate the taste of mint. There was to be a party, at her parents' tennis club, in the evening, and I'd need a change of clothes for that. Mum rolled my favourite dress to save it from creasing. I took out Joey the stuffed dog; he was for someone much younger than nine.

Kat lived a few streets away, which was a big distance in that small town. From our row of terraces, my mum walked me to Kat's home. The road flowered into this wide cul-de-sac crowned with detached bungalows and sloping lawns. Kat ran out to meet me; she must have been waiting at the window. I was too excited to do much more than leap up and down, releasing myself from my mum's grip. The grass felt springy beneath my pumps. This was going to be my new wonderful life: a friend to sit with, a friend to share secrets with. In many ways, those predictions came true.

My mum turned and waved as she walked off.

'I'm so pleased you're here,' Kat said.

She carried my plastic bag with one hand like it was a carton of fragile eggs. My face ached from smiling. Her free arm swung at her side, fingertips brushing mine as we walked into the bungalow. I thought she must want me to hold her dangling hand.

I was right because she didn't tug herself free when I did. Kat held on tight.

'Shh,' she said. 'Mum's having a lie-down.'

There didn't seem to be enough light inside. Nets up, curtains half-drawn. I thought that's what people in bungalows must do when anyone could walk past and glance in.

We tiptoed to the bedroom door. Her mum lay curled on the bed like something from a fairy tale: pink slippers neatly placed at the side; hair spread over the silk ruffled pillow.

'I put some new ribbons in your room,' her mum said without lifting her head. 'Dad gets back at six. We have to be ready for then.'

'Shh,' Kat whispered again to me or her mum; it wasn't clear which.

The door clicked shut behind us.

Kat and me played outside. There weren't really any rules to the game; we just took it in turns to have a scarf tied around our heads and run up the grassy slope, guided by the other's calls. Spring called too. A liquid heat in the air like breathing in the steam from warmed milk. We ran up and down. The next-door neighbour's lawn was encircled by thick beds of tulips and daffodils. It was hard not to stray onto his striped grass.

He watched from the bay window the first time Kat stumbled onto his lawn. When Kat took her next turn and trod in the flowerbed, he stood on his porch. He wore khaki shorts, his legs were thin, or his knees were swollen, hard to tell which. He had on a matching short-sleeved jacket as if he was about to go on a bear hunt. When Kat tied the scarf about my face, ready for another spin, I heard him come crunching down the gravel driveway. I turned my head; through the pinprick holes in the fabric, sunlight fell to darkness. He stood in front of Kat.

'Don't trample the flowers,' the old neighbour said. 'Run off and play somewhere else.'

There didn't seem much point to the game anymore. We went inside to get ready for the party. Kat held up the packet of hair ribbons. Red, blue, and yellow strands were plaited together, each secured with a silver bobble on the end.

'One for you. One for me,' Kat said.

But no matter how we tried, we couldn't get it to clip straight in my wiry hair. The bobble hung at an angle, knocking against my ear. I scratched my scalp, ready to pluck it out. Kat shook her head. I let my hand drop.

'Don't upset Mum,' she said. 'She got them especially.'

Kat put on her new jeans, flowers stitched on the knee, and a silver blouse; cuffs and collar embroidered in black. I flapped out my dress, not a crease to be seen, but I wanted to scrunch it up and throw it away. Kat said the green check was pretty, but I knew I'd got the party invitation wrong. It was a disco. That night was to be my first.

Kat's parents sat near the bar, laughing and drinking on a table for two. When we went near them, her mum tried to shoo us away. Kat leaned against her dad.

He patted her hair. 'Don't you look pretty,' he said. Draping the trailing ribbons and beads between his fingers.

'We both have them,' Kat said, pointing to the side of my head.

He smiled, said, 'Two colas coming up for the twins.'

He returned from the bar, glasses clinking with ice and bobbing with lemon slices.

Kat's mum said, 'Why don't you go and dance?' It wasn't really a question.

Kat took my hand, rushed me down corridors in the tennis club. I didn't pay enough attention to the directions to be able to find my way out again, too busy trying not to spill a precious drop (at home we didn't have fizzy pop).

It might as well have been another world in that room. Flashing lights on the stage, tape music playing on a loop. We had the place to ourselves, stood with our knees touching the low stage. The thudding bass trembled through my limbs into the glass clenched between my hands.

Kat did three enormous burps. I twisted my mouth, dug with my tongue, but no sound came out. She was the champion, and I was defeated.

But out on the empty dance floor, we weren't anything but bright energy, to glide and slide, to feel, for moments at a time, that we might giddily spin up and away.

'Catch me,' Kat yelled. She dropped to her knees, propelled herself across the polished wooden boards.

We ended up in a tangled heap on the carpet surrounding the dance floor. The adults started to come in, drinking and laughing. Kat and I stayed out of the way, careful not to get trodden on.

It got late; headlights slid across the windows. A drink got spilled. Kat lost a ribbon, and it was declared time to leave. But Kat wanted one more cola. Kat wanted one more song. Kat wanted to see her parents dance; she pushed them together.

'Don't worry. We'll all come again,' Kat's dad said. He put an arm around our shoulders, led us out to the car.

My teeth were slick with cola. I worked hard with the pink brush and strawberry paste to swish it all away. Kat used the bathroom next, leaving me to get changed into my nightie. I wasn't sure if I should leave my knickers on or not; I'd never slept at someone else's house before. I decided it would be politer to leave them on.

Kat's bed was against the wall, her pillow by the door. The main light shone bright, reflecting off the white wardrobes on the other wall. An inflatable mattress lay tucked under the window. I fingered the pottery frogs standing to attention on the chest of drawers, each positioned to face the door like they kept watch.

The light went out. I knocked a frog, catching it before it felled the rest like dominoes. Darkness for a moment before the table lamp snapped awake. Kat's dad stood by the bed. He didn't quite close the door, still space for a hand to slip through.

He tapped the pillows. 'Hop in,' he said.

Kat's stuffed bear grinned; her Raggedy Anne doll stared. I pushed them to the wall, slid under the duvet. The sheet was wrinkled, gritty from use. Water gurgled in the bathroom pipes. A cough vibrated through the wall. He sat on the edge of the bed. I rolled a little towards the dent. He lowered his head.

And he kissed me.

His chin and cheeks looked smooth but felt like the steel pronged comb my mum used on my wet hair. I stared like the doll, mouth sealed in a grin like the bear. His tongue pushed through the narrow line of my lips. A last breath of toothpaste on my tongue but not like the strawberry flavour in my bag: I tasted mint. He withdrew.

'Kat likes it,' he said, still tilted over me, a whole ceiling of Day-Glo stars winking behind him.

Kat opened the door, back from the bathroom. He tucked the duvet tight about me. I couldn't move.

Kat crawled over the inflatable mattress on the floor. The plastic made a croaking sound like alarmed frogs. She turned her face to the wall. He put out the light, left us alone with a galaxy of fast fading stars littered across the ceiling.

Somebody said, the middle of a story *is* the story, but sometimes in the middle things just go on as they always have. You go home to your mum and your annoying brother, you say you had a nice time sleeping over at Kat's, you say you're invited again another week, and sometimes there are different friends, and then there is a different school, but really you and your best friend Kat only exist for each other. And before the lights go out is just a secret time and nothing much happens and you tell yourself it's just a kiss and your best friend never talks of it which must mean it's really nothing at all because you speak of everything else. So, it is never spoken of, not that, not the nights week after week she's alone in that room with the frogs, waiting for her dad to turn out the light. Only middles can't go on and on and on...

Half-way through the first year of GCSEs, Kat plucked her eyebrow hairs into a thin dark line – it was a fashion of sorts. A few weeks later she set to work on her eyelashes too. When she came into school that day, lids white and puffy, I knew we were somewhere towards the end of things. The school trip was my idea, something to do, something to take us away for a day at least.

And it always, this story, ends up back at Hyde Park.

Traffic snaking its slow path, the red bus leaving us behind. We dropped down in the grass and bushes. Clouds of skunk grazed the tree branches above. Mouths lubricated by cheap larger. Getting so high, so very high. The secret was far below, and the sun was shining, and the joint was strong enough to numb my legs. I leaned over, rested my head on Kat's lap, ran my fingertip around the green lines on the base of her fingers.

Why would I let myself fall asleep?

Why would I leave her alone?

Kat never came back to school. She didn't take any exams. Someone said she stayed in London to work as an au pair; I couldn't say for sure if that was true. With Kat gone, it was much easier to forget about those small, pale, bald eyelids, and the row of fragile porcelain frogs. But that old neighbour sometimes still appeared in my dreams, whispering not shouting, as if addressing someone he'd known for years, 'Don't trample the flowers.'

I run, in those dreams, no pain, like the grace marathon runners reach when everything hums as a machine, and they know they can go and go, and go. It feels like flying.

I run now too. Half marathons, 10K park runs. I get placed sometimes, never quite a win. It's the acceptable face of self-harm. I'm too much of a coward to cut myself, to have people inspecting my wounds.

I don't visit my mum much – she still lives in that small town – and I don't ask questions, not even of Google. I've never typed Kat's name into any search engine. I don't deserve to find relief there, and any pain couldn't be worse than what I've already seen in idle moments gazing out of train windows, losing myself in an Excel spreadsheet, screaming out of a deep (but not deep enough) sleep – I've seen all the things that can happen to a fifteen-year-old girl.

Although, again, I prove myself at fault – I came close to saying her name once.

One Christmas, a couple of years after university, I was in the car with my mum and brother, sitting in the backseat – perhaps that's what made me feel like a child again. As we drove through the estate, hitting road bumps, leaving my stomach suspended in the air for moments at a time, acid swelled inside, and words bubbled up like a cola burp. I told my mum and brother about some girl I'd gone to school with, that someone said her dad had been arrested for child abuse.

They studied me in the rear-view mirror, questioned me, uttered warnings about rumour mills and cruel gossip, how things could get twisted in the repeating. I looked out of the window: *objects in mirror are closer than they appear.* They asked me again if it could really be true.

What happened, all those years ago, was only a moment balanced before the light goes out and darkness kisses you, when nothing is real, and everything is terrible.

I answered, 'No, it's just something somebody said.'

I tried telling the policewoman. I tried telling my family. Now I'm telling you.

I don't expect to be believed. The story never quite runs right in my head, trips over itself, falls down at any probing as if I'm waking again each time – alone in Hyde Park, knowing from the scattered blue cans and grey roaches that it... something... happened... but always left with nothing.

So I smoke, and I run marathons; I see no reason to make the training easier on myself. Or maybe I'm just too weak to stop – stop the weed – and do what? Stand still and let it all come running at me? I like the sting in my shins, the throb in my feet, the thudding in my lungs, and I never stop, keep going, aiming out beyond the pain for the moment of bursting lightness when...

I close my eyes, see her gently lifting my head. See her kissing me softly on the cheek (as a child should be kissed). See one of the men offer his hand, helping to haul her up. See her glancing back at me, at that school uniform, at that small-town life, at all that ever was...

Run, Kat, run.

A Match

They sit in the walled garden; she and he. The summer sun slips behind the Victorian terraced houses. She on one side of the marble-topped table, he on the other.

The night comes swiftly, unfolding itself from the bricks of the city. He pulls a box from his pocket, shakes it before opening. One left.

The candle sits between them.

She lifts her camera, the cool plastic of the viewfinder against her skin. It is an old-fashioned Cannon, with dials and without digital displays.

He strikes the match, trailing a flame of yellow and orange across her lens. She refocuses, drawing whiteness out of the sulphurous blackness. Her finger turning the dial. Increasing aperture.

His face waits: chiaroscuro.

The moth in her dancing, circling, towards his light.

Her finger presses.

Her heart snaps.

Much more than a snapshot – a match.

Beginnings and Endings

Begin here, the canonical five: Mary Ann Nichols; Annie Chapman; Elizabeth Stride; Catherine Eddowes; Mary Jane Kelly.

Now, before them comes another.

Above the rooftops of Whitechapel, the sky smoulders, clouds of purple smother the last of the bank holiday fun, balanced in this August night, 1888. A brackish redness, the tincture of twilight, trickles like laudanum through the streets, empty but for remnants of feathers and beads from the fair; drifting but finding no rest.

A woman enters George Yard Buildings. Martha Tabram (if she owed rent then she'd give her name as Emma) is not alone. She grabs the man's arm as they climb the stairs. Gin and ale make her legs weak. Just about merry enough to imagine she's off to bed. *Lead us not into temptation, but deliver us from evil.* It's far too late for night-time prayers.

She lifts her foot to take another step. He draws her back. Presses her arms to her sides. Thrusts his cheek into her neck, whispers something. It tickles. Laugh and this business will take all night. He unbuttons his coat, opens his arms. Martha leans into his left side. If she were on the right, she'd feel the knife in his pocket.

This is a story with many beginnings but only one ending. There is only ever one ending, ever.

Dawn brings a new beginning, or the same old beginning always waiting for another ending. There's one here who, if not sleeping nor resting, is certainly done.

Martha dies against the wall of George Yard Buildings, a step further – there, on the first landing. Some have already stepped over her. It's dark and damp. They'd be forgiven for not seeing the thick pools of blood, the thrown-up skirts and pale exposed shins. But she's there, in the midst of it. Her legs kicked apart.

A graze marks her left knee where she was knocked to the floor. But they'll not notice that. Her body is punctured and slit. Life runs out of her. She can't rest yet. She has to be poked, measured, drained, and cut deeper on the wooden table waiting for her at the dead house.

Her dark hair and brows, cheekbones that hold her features high, keep her young-looking even this close to her end. Her mouth is open. Her hair has threads of gold. Her lips are swollen with gin. Her eyelids flutter, not as in sleep, but like a child refusing to look, believing, *If I can't see you, you're not there.*

Martha's eyes will be wide open when they do find her body. Some will hope to find captured on that lens the last face she saw. They'll find nothing of course. But all will come to know him that killed her, although there's a little longer to wait for his moniker – Jack the Ripper. He'll have more beginnings than anyone: newspaper headlines, saucy postcards, waxworks shows, comics and paperbacks, and when film is invented, he'll have many faces and voices. But all that is yet to come.

There's no helping Martha, leave her be. Although she might help others if they could hear the warning. She could tell how love is for sale on these streets. Choose from any colour, age, sex, or girth. From any sale there's money to be got. Martha saw how her stock sank the more she drank. But remember the value and the cost of a thing isn't the same as its price in shillings and pennies.

Daylight is coming, but it won't lift this darkness.

If these aren't the sorts of beginnings for you, then wait a while, for little children up on the moor, or girls in matching football shirts off for a stroll, those women with tracks on their arms out beckoning for cars and trouble: missing, snatched, strangled, tortured – beginning on beginning, there'll be more tomorrow – so many to choose from.

But for now, back to that canonical five...

Mary Ann Nichols, or Polly (as she uses when thinking of herself), is struck with the memory of her children as she watches a mother, father, and daughter walk by. Now there's no denying Polly's had a hard time of things, and whether you think this her own fault through the drinking, or whether you've pity enough to think all them little 'uns and the husband she can't stand but when drunk (and that's what led to all the offspring) is plenty of reason to seek gin. Well, she's on her way to the alehouse now.

When she has enough inside, Polly feels brave as a lion. With the burn of it in her throat, she knows how easy it is to earn doss money. With the metallic bite of it on her tongue, she knows there's nothing to fear from those men she takes. Seed and gin, they've both got a tang to them. Both good for face-making too. But only when she's enough drink inside her does she see the faces of her children. There's the rub. It's still early enough in the day for her to feel the bitter pinch of that – like that mother, preacher father, and daughter there – Polly's youngest must be about that age.

She looks up, a tapping noise behind a window of St Botolph's roots her for a moment. Is it a sign? Jesus let whores wash his feet. Mary laughs, knows she's not likely to meet him on the streets of Whitechapel. There's no one can save her. Not even her own father.

She thinks of the letter she wrote him not a month before, about her new position, about the very good people who gave her employment, teetotallers and religious. Oh, but didn't they deserve to be brought a little low, to feel some prick of pain, at what they let into their home.

When she stole the Zouave jacket, the bonnets, the embroidered underskirts, and the red, spotted handkerchief, she pretended that wearing those things would make her the woman she always thought she could be. She went and sold them of course; except the little black bonnet which she wears.

What does Mary think of herself now, stooping to the cobbles, pocketing a tortoiseshell comb with only a few prongs missing? She's probably got a head bubbling with longings, doubts, and fears, not so different from yours. Stop and ask her. But do it fast as it's the last chance there will be.

A few streets over, two men prop Martha against the dead house wall as if in death she has more substance than she ever had in life. They fasten a clamp to her neck. Martha is set hard, but she'll start to sour then slacken if she's not put under soon. For now, a man gets out his measuring stick. He pushes a block against her feet to hold her.

The other man widens the legs of the studio camera, lowers the focus; they make a joke of this. But there is something wrong with the plate; it won't capture what it should. The men tap and fiddle with the camera. The body slips against the green-tiled wall but doesn't fall.

A moment of balance, like the day that started with such bank holiday fun. If Martha hadn't taken that arm, if she hadn't agreed a price, hadn't turned her back to steady herself...

The men give up on the camera; they won't capture her likeness. They take out pencils, scales and tapes. Nothing that they note will portray Martha's being. The light fades quickly.

A little rain. Those out on the street stand under the London plane tree; it offers some protection. Worse will follow.

Find shelter where you can.

Summer breaks itself over the Ends; rumbling thunder, lightning, heralding a September of grey skies and early frosts. The turn of the season gusts away dandelions in cracks and birds in the sky. The high winter tides will swamp the hot stink of the city, the flotsam and jetsam shipwrecked on Thames mud banks. But the last hours of August still blaze bright.

Flames sweep high over Shadwell dry dock, washing the East End red. The fire draws more and more people, bundled together like kindling. Smoke laps the road, hauling the smell of blackened oak and bone over them all. Those that believe in such cleansings, and even those that don't, think it must bring hope that the darkness of Martha Tabram's bloody gutting was only some summer madness. They're wrong; it burns a false dawn.

A speck of ash descends from the sky, settling on Mary's arm. Morning is a long way off. All the prayer rooms are closed, and all good folks are abed... This is London, not some milk-fed, apple-picking, honeybee-buzzing village. Although there's still shit everywhere – watch where you tread.

Mary Ann Nichols knew this corner of the Ends, its hard edges, and its knocks. She's surprisingly soft though, to the touch. Here, take a handful.

Or take her hand, the fingers resting, curled up against the gate which she'll never pass through now. See the bruise on either cheek – he took her face in his hands, gentle pressure at first, as if to kiss. Perhaps she turned her head aside or sniffed. He pressed harder, tried to crush her. That must have shocked her some, but she'd had worse.

Only when the knife came out did she fear what was coming. No voice to cry, all the words oozing out of the gash in her neck. She might have thought him a thief even then, because she'd been done that way before. She's no fool.

If anything can be sold it can also be stolen: clothes, gold, hearts, but can a life be stolen? Doesn't stolen mean it's still out there, still somewhere just not with its owner?

A bonnet lies on the ground. A neat little black one left behind in the mud and the blood. Don't worry, it's not needed anymore.

The dock fire is out. A storm has washed the Ends black. Cinder and the last of the rain drips down windows and faces. Ashes to ashes, dust to dust – people on the street say that to each other; buying newspapers or stopping to hear the ragged paperboys call out, *Murder! Murder!* They know their numbers – there has been another. No news but that for weeks.

Voices on the corner, telling all who pass that they saw Mary Ann Nichols only hours before she got sliced, not the last to see her mind, no need to get caught up in police business.

An invading army of coppers and toffs marches past the shop fronts. Popinjays each and every one. Never has so much fine leather, and so many carefully turned walking canes, been seen on the Whitechapel Road.

Some scribble with pencils. *It could be him. She could be next.* Studying faces like mud scraped off with a stick. An Inspector strides along, trailing two Hampstead types (stout boots, fur-trimmed coats, rosy cheeks). He stops by a coster stall. The pie woman glances up, rusty liquor-ladle in hand.

The Inspector says, 'Seen any tall hat, black-bag carrying strangers lately, mother?'

She shakes her head.

The wife says to her husband, 'Is that woman really the Inspector's mother?'

But the Inspector gets in first. 'Shouldn't I be ashamed if it were? Mother is an expression about these parts.'

The couple walks on, peers into the mouth of a dangerously dark alley, probably hoping to catch sight of bloody boot prints; not thinking about the mothers, the sisters, the daughters.

Crowds swell, washing up against shops and front doors, looks like the whole of London has turned out for this funeral procession. Lining the street, blinds half-drawn, coppers wearing polished boots. This isn't for royalty, nor any Prime Minister, not even some much-loved vaudeville type. The East End is here for one of its own: Mary Ann Nichols. Pity she's a whore – is that what they're thinking?

Three men walk behind the coffin – father, once was husband, and son. Behind them, and around them, is half the city. A small girl in a striped apron waves a flag. No one tells her to put it away. The peanut sellers and sweet trays are doing brisk trade.

There's many who claim to have liked Mary, many more who'll say, What a good heart she had. Well, now they're treading on each other, hanging out of windows, getting an eyeful for free. And just see the shine on that fine polished elm. Mary's not in that box, though her body is. Depending who you ask, you'll get a different answer about where she is.

Him that finished her off will never see so many at his end. But the grand words, the painted pictures, will all be his. A girl with black ribbons trimming her hat, says what many are thinking: Mary's a lucky one, to be noticed now, as she never was in life. Her name won't linger long, although she collects a few other titles over the years: prostitute; victim.

Maybe you think it too – those sorts of women aren't due a happy ending. Only, watching this beginning of a show, you've missed another end...

Now here's something new. Who's in the shell? It bumps along the road, on its way to the dead house. And don't go thinking it's Mary Ann Nichols – time has moved on; a lifetime can be lived in a week. Although that is the same shell that Mary lay in.

The wooden slats are weathered as a ship's hull, one too cracked to be seaworthy. As the cart makes its slow procession through another crowd, anyone could slip a finger between the planks: cloth, skin, blood, and bone. All once belonged to Annie Chapman before her end.

The cart passes, people step out of the way. Annie's not much of a load. But fatty is what they'll call her in their reports. She hasn't eaten much for days, for weeks. Food fell apart, tasted like sand in her mouth. Her body is a blister, like she'd swish and slosh when walking; skin lifting off her. She's sick, so sick and tired. Death went and freed her from that.

She's just like any other here on the street that you'd pass without a second look. But you're probably wondering how *he* picks them. Luck or judgement? There's a newspaperman over there, in tweed and wool, who's brewing a name for him. It'll be written down soon, just wait – *Jack the Ripper* is about to be christened in ink. But there's someone else watching.

He's in the crowd. He knows he should have got far away, but silent as Annie is, she still calls to him. Hear it? The clink clink of brass rings in his pocket, no longer warm from Annie's skin, cold as old fish bones.

He'll not be seen. Plenty have seen him of course, but no one knows it's him. That's part of why he smiles sometimes when buying a roasted potato with extra salt or catches his breath if someone passes too close on the street. He's a showman without greasepaint, a newspaperman without ink.

It's a bloody performance.

A Noiseless Midnight Terror the newspapers call it, but there isn't much silent about Whitechapel. Each day has an end but only if sleep is found can that next new day begin. Hunting for sleep, hearing bells instead – St Saviours, St Olave's, St Dunstan's, St Boltoph, Spitalfields – an echo of chimes marking their different hours, singing out: *She is dead*. Harmonising into the childhood song:

> *When will that be?*
> *Say the bells of Stepney.*
> *I do not know,*
> *Says the great bell at Bow.*
> *Here comes a candle to light you to bed,*
> *And here comes a chopper to chop off your head!*

It is going to be a long, long night.

The first to be found is Elizabeth Stride. They think she's drunk, which was true (she'd have to be, wouldn't she, to be out in such times), but that isn't why she lies so still in the yard. Stand back a little, don't step in the blood, that way trouble lies. The red and white rose pinned to her collar can still be seen. Although it's all red now. Before the last striking of the clock, those petals were white as St Paul's dome (not like it is now but as it once was when new); a bright beacon in a dark place, that flower – well worth the fourpence Elizabeth paid.

Some might think she should have put up a fight: scream, shout, beg. Elizabeth was silenced. Her windpipe slashed. But

the cut is only on one side. Ever seen a slaughterman drain a hog? He knows how to rush the blood out of it, to do it quick. Perhaps a nick to the throat isn't such a bad way to go. Before anyone calls her the lucky one of the night, stop, count to one hundred and eighty seven: ....
....
....
.... (Did you count each one?)

That's how long it took Elizabeth Stride, in silence, to die. It will take much longer for anyone to name her, and the list is growing. No one has the heart for a funeral procession. Long Liz will make that last long journey into the mud of the East London Cemetery at Plaistow without friends or family beside her.

Now she's alone too, there's nothing but the low whistle of the wind, like the hiss of a draught under a door, hushed and cold. Only there's no rest to be had. Quick, quick, catch him working his way through the next. The second of the night is alive but knows she dies. Hurry, head west, towards Mitre Square.

It's not yet two in the morning; darkness stretches out in this lee between dusk and dawn. The city loosens the clenched muscles of its thoroughfares and dead ends. This is his time, or so he thinks. But he carries another with him. Elizabeth's blood sticks to his soles, travelled to this spot in Mitre Square. With a swing of his arm, the scythe of the knife, he's enjoying it.

This here, down on the ground, is Catherine Eddowes. Remember that because he's about to try and make you forget.

Not content with killing Catherine, he works to turn her inside out, like an artist destroys a canvas so that no one else might look on it.

Cutting, slicing, nicking, tearing through skin and intestine. V-cuts below her eyes. Her lids diced. Her nose hacked back to the bone. He's got time to work at this one.

Catherine lies on her back, in a spreading pool of her own blood.

Look away, and he might just stop – for now. But he's not finished yet.

'End Times. End Times,' a man shouts, marching up and down, ringing a handbell. Declaring the end to be nigh, loud as any Friday night newspaper seller: the prophecies have been cast, the plagues sweeping over London, striking down the ungodly.

The man turns. 'Are you saved?'

He rubs a sleeve across his eyes; maybe he isn't even sure there's anyone there. He shakes his head, trudges on. A bundle of children starts pelting him with stones and sticks. He tries to run, but the boards roped over his shoulders hobble him. He limps away, back hunched against the blows, heading towards Aldgate East like an unwilling Pied Piper. He thinks he can save them from some evil beginnings, but then he's not the only liar to be met on these streets.

Winter arrives the next day, too early in the month. The cobbles of Commercial Street are prettied with frost. Button up shirts, tuck in neckerchiefs, secure any loose flap before the wind bites. Folks shrink into themselves, but it isn't just the weather. A coster wheels his barrel up Flower and Dean, a boy runs across his path, swiping an orange. The man just shakes his head, keeps on going, eyes down. It wouldn't do to get denounced – *It's him! Murderer!*

No woman is safe, so the newspapers say.

They have a name for him now that tingles on the tongue and stands up on the page: Jack the Ripper. There are even some, who for a fit, sign themselves *The Ripper, Saucy Jack, Jack the lad*. Others put red pencil to cheap paper, scribble down their fantasies, send them out into the world, all for the price of a stamp. *Dear Boss – Catch me when you can*.

There are some so lunatic in their own mind, they truly believe themselves to be the murderer. There are others who can't look away from Old Jackie and his deeds, read each line, each word, each letter, as if all those black smudges could reveal who he is: he's learned; he's illiterate; he's obviously a pauper; a rich man; a prince; a doctor; a butcher. There's even some claim the killer must be a midwife. What lovely imagery that would be – the bringer of life and death! Beginnings and endings swaddled together.

Open the papers, find them there: Catherine Eddowes, Elizabeth Stride, Annie Chapman, Mary Ann Nichols, Martha Tabram, each stuck like a pin to the page. Their faces trapped in small circles as if ready to be cut up for a keepsake locket. Eyes closed, mouths loose, caught with a last breath on their lips. There are more last breaths to come.

Meet Mary Jane Kelly. She tells any that listen about the winters in Ireland and Wales, although she never gives the same story twice. Sometimes Marie Jeanette or Mary Ann, Fair Emma. There's more truth in her songs, and Mary does love to sing. Her mother told her once, That pretty voice is your crowning glory. And Mary held to that long after she'd been discarded by them all.

She's sitting in the Ten Bells with a song buzzing on the tip of her tongue. Sometimes she thinks she has bees in her mouth, and if she doesn't sing the sting will burn right through her. The song in her head is, 'A Violet from Mother's Grave'.

And oft' times when I'm sad at heart,
this flow'r has given me joy,
But while life does remain, in memoriam I'll retain
This small violet I plucked from mother's grave.

Only the pub isn't so busy, no one asks for a tune. The landlady puts a beer down for Mary. She thinks about waving it away, the drink from yesterday had given her the horrors; it still scalded the back of her throat. But what else is she to do in a pub if not drink, they don't allow idlers. Mary takes the beer over to a couple of old girls she recognises from around Miller's Court.

There's no time these days for 'hellos' and 'how is yous', all talk starts the same:

'Police say they're on the Ripper's tail alright.'

'Can't find their own tails, more like.'

'Lost a bloodhound, so I hear it.'

'They'll be more, wait and see.'

'The Jews are the ones—'

'No, no – "The Juwes are the ones won't be blamed for nothing".'

'Is it them or not?'

'How should I know. Bloody coppers scrubbed the writing off the wall.'

'Suppose we'll never know.'

'I know a nice tailor, he's one of them, good with his hands.'

The old birds set to chattering about men they've known, and men they've lost. The barman shakes his head at such low ways. Live bad, die bad – isn't that what he's thinking? Lower that nose. Who hasn't lost their head over some unsuitable fancy? The only difference is luck. Lucky enough to hide a bruised heart, to sail on with life. There's no applause here.

Mary drains the last of the beer. She'll have to move on.

Don't try calling out a warning. Mary can't hear – not above the drum of the street, the hum in her head. What could be said that she doesn't already know? There's a murderer about, watch out! But move closer, step a little lighter – hear the tune she's carrying as she heads for the river:

> *The vows we made to heav'n above*
> *shall ever cheer and bind me.*
> *In constancy to her I love,*
> *the girl I left behind me.*

Although Mary has left many things behind her, she still carries a heavy load that can never be put down. She's a set of shoulders on her, and a wide back, so she won't be caught stooping. But in her dreams, she curls small as a kitten, breathes in the steam of bubbling cabbage and frying onions – the scent of home.

She's come to the docks for a roasted potato. The potato man doesn't need to shout. The smoke rises high, signalling to the hungry. She sniffs the hot coals. The metal bucket glows red.

Mary peels off strips of the leathery skin with her teeth, holding the warm whiteness in her hands. She watches the boats as she eats. Tea clippers, steamers, sails rolling open, breaking through the mist like birds surfacing above a forest. Bails hoisted high in the air, swinging towards warehouse mouths. The tinkle of rigging and ropes, the bubble of foreign voices.

Those new arrivals reach land with wobbling legs, carrying not much more than the mud on their boots. They're from old countries – deep mountains, blackened mining towns, barren fields, dry rivers – that have spat them out like fish bones, across dark seas to other waiting plates.

London sits with her arms open but her lap full. This city isn't to blame or praise for anything to come. Stone and brick and mud run through it; the blood is all ours. As the gulls cry, circling overhead – Good luck to you all, is what Mary Jane Kelly longs to sing.

Night falls fast. A bright spark glows in the alley up ahead. Someone still kept awake, kept out of sight. The bowl of a pipe glowing redder with each breath.

The footsteps stop. A hollow knocking echoes off the wet bricks; sparks falling to ash. Maybe he has retreated deeper into the alley – back to bed, back to work. The darkness tugs.

Is it the Ripper?

Don't get excited; he's not going to turn and show his face. Though he's close enough that those bloodhounds the police are trialling could wag their tails and strike him. But there are other bloodhounds all around. Those who love to tut and hang their heads, well-up with pity. Those tucking hands into pockets, leaning back on their heels, flushed warm with smugness. Those lost to the thrill of it all, standing together, intent as them listening to betting odds and fingering a lucky rabbit's foot: *It'd never happen to me or mine; they had it coming.*

To hell with them all.

Is he from hell? Something stirs, dark coat flapping like a bird's wing. Shadows swell and subside in the alley.

There goes the lord of misrule. Does the ground open up a pit of fallen angels and jigging devils for him? Does fire blaze from his fingers?

Tommyrot, he's just a man. Now, that's a thought sure to keep you awake at night. Click click of the pipe against a wall, a nail being flicked against teeth. A chuckle?

Not a light comes on in the street.

Sooner or later an end always comes, always the same end. She dies. She dies. She dies, she dies. She dies. All things end.

One thing of which there can be no doubt: no one wants the end that's waiting for Mary Kelly. If you don't believe it, look for yourself.

Mary's watching too. Call it a dream, a vision, a split, a religious fervour, but Mary looks down on herself in these final moments. From above, in the corner, beside that tattered hanging print of a weeping widow, Mary watches. She was sleeping. Now she is here. Cut jaggedly out of herself.

Perhaps you're relieved by that; it must mean she won't feel the slice through her breasts, deep down to the lung, or the stab in her thigh, the stripping back of flesh. Come now, haven't you been guided by the hand? Take a step on your own. She knows all that is happening, even though the place is dark, the halfpenny candle nearly out.

There's no chorus for the dying in this room. No end songs. The last of the flame balances in the broken wine glass on the table. One minute left. And it's a longer lifetime than Mary Kelly's ever lived.

Take another step; you've come this far. How close will you go to get what you want? Will you watch through the window? Will your breath fog the cracked pane? Reach through that hole, unlatch the door. Get close enough for blood drops to splash your shoes. Lie on that bed. Tilt back your head. Open your legs – all to see his face. To lay claim, I know who Jack the Ripper is. Would you?

There's the briefest of chances left, between the light going out and her heart being dug out. He won't notice the moment at which Mary dies, but then to him she was never a life.

Go on, let yourself in. Unmask him, name him, lay claim to that glory. His is a story to live on, begin again and again, long after hers has ended. Hers? Do you even remember her name?

Prostitute – it's not a proper name; victim neither. Well, if you know each of these women (only six of so so many), if you can recite their given names – not to bring them back, but only to hold them close for a moment before releasing them – then stay a little longer.

If not, then what business is this of yours. Go, your time here is at an end.

ACKNOWLEDGEMENTS

I'd like to thank Deirdre and Robin for their feedback on many of these stories. I'd also like to thank Joe Melia at the Bristol Short Story Prize for his continued support of my writing and the short story form.

~

The author and publisher wish to thank the editors of the publications in which the following stories were first published:

'My Girl' was first published in the *Bristol Short Story Prize Anthology*, July 2011; 'Tombstoning' – *The Mechanic's Institute Review*, November 2017; 'Zoom' – *Bath Short Story Award Anthology*, October 2014; 'Dinner Dance' – *Molatov Cocktail*, May 2011; 'Freshwater' – *A Short Affair* (Scribner), Royal Academy & Pin Drop Short Story Award 2017, Shortlisted, July 2018; 'Human Terrain' – *Bookanista*, April 2014; 'On Broadway' – *Remembering Oluwale: An Anthology* (Valley Press), June 2016; 'They Were the Only Ones Dancing' – *May You: The Walter Swan Memorial Anthology* (Valley Press), May 2018; 'Open House' – *Brick Lane Bookshop Short Story Prize Anthology*, October 2019.

REFLEX PRESS

Reflex Press is an independent publisher based in Abingdon, Oxfordshire, committed to publishing bold and innovative books by emerging authors from across the UK and beyond.

Since our inception in 2018, we have published award-winning short story collections, flash fiction anthologies, and novella-length fiction.

www.reflex.press
@reflexfiction